LEAVING 2020

Geoff Woliner

Copyright © 2020 Geoff Woliner

"All rights reserved. No part of this book may be reproduced in any form or by any electronic or mechanical means, including information storage and retrieval systems, without written permission from the author, except in the case of a reviewer, who may quote brief passages embodied in critical articles or in a review. Trademarked names appear throughout this book. Rather than use a trademark symbol with every occurrence of a trademarked name, names are used in an editorial fashion, with no intention of infringement of the respective owner's trademark. The information in this book is distributed on an "as is" basis, without warranty. Although every precaution has been taken in the preparation of this work, neither the author nor the publisher shall have any liability to any person or entity with respect to any loss or damage caused or alleged to be caused directly or indirectly by the information contained in this book."

ISBN: 978-1-7331259-9-4

CONTENTS

- CONTENTS iii
- ACKNOWLEDGMENTS 1
- Prologue 2
- Chapter 1: The Ultimate Decision 3
- Chapter 2: Mermaids and Magic 18
- Chapter 3: The Jewel of India 42
- Chapter 4: Nothing and Everything 58
- Chapter 5: The Waves of Marbella 73
- Chapter 6: The Birth of a Rebellion 86
- Chapter 7: Chasing Waterfalls 102
- Chapter 8: Feeling the Love 118
- Chapter 9: Punts, Pints and Pitches 144
- Chapter 10: Elephants and Amaretto 144
- Chapter 11: BBQ and Corn 177
- Chapter 12: THE FINAL DESTINATION 199
- ABOUT THE AUTHOR 216

LEAVING 2020

ACKNOWLEDGMENTS

In the summer of 2020, I had a crazy idea (which fit like a glove in 2020).

What if I could crowdsource a book?

I would simply put out a call, see who responded, and then take whatever random submissions I received and cobble together a book.

To my surprise, the response was incredible. I received submissions by the dozens. People from all over the world responded with their *stories, hopes, dreams, passions* and *offbeat rants*.

Your tales, thoughts and struggles formed the nucleus of an idea, which then birthed this journey.

In no particular order, my deepest, most heartfelt gratitude goes to all of you who contributed to make this book a reality:

Mel, Mirrie, Shanthi, Binati, Ashish, Ana-Maria, Kelsey, Helen, Greg, Judy, Sue, Aman, Harmeet, Violeta, Siala, Darren, Barnali, Caroline, Eric, Keith, Tom (Fitz), Sarah, Edna, Alysandrah, Brian, Ritvik, Liz, Tal, Sabriya, Jane, Paige, Tetyana, Carina, Margaret, David, Carolynn, and Andrea.

I love you all and can never thank you enough.

May your stories inspire others on their journeys.

Prologue

April 30th, 2020.

That was the last day of my life.

You were there.

Yes, you.

I know.

You think I'm crazy and have you confused with someone else.

But I don't. It's you. It's always been you.

You are the key to everything. Even if you may not remember.

So, I'm asking you to bear with me, because this may not make much sense.

I experienced it, at least I think I did, and I know you experienced it with me too.

So, I'm going to walk you through it all. The 30th of April. And everything that came afterwards.

...and I pray that you remember. That it somehow all comes back to you. Because, again, you are the key to everything.

You're the only one who can help me.

You're the only one who can help them.

You're the only one who can help us all.

Chapter 1: The Ultimate Decision

"So, are you going to jump?"

I wasn't sure how to answer this particular question. I wanted to jump, more than anything. It was time.

Ashish asked again, "So, are you going to jump?"

I sat in frozen, suspended animation as he stared me down. He was going to get his answer. He wasn't leaving without one.

It was 11:50 p.m. on April 30th, 2020. I made my way to the roof of my apartment building on the Lower East Side of Manhattan.

It was my time to go. This was the only way. This was going to be the last day of my life.

I made a pact with myself on April 1st. I was finally done.

I was done after two hellish weeks of lockdown in this shitty apartment with thin walls and neighbors who wouldn't shut up. Arguing, fighting, yelling, slamming doors, slamming walls. *God*, I hated them.

I was done after losing my job as a journalist for The *Herald* where, believe it or not, I actually made some decent bank for the first time in my life.

I couldn't believe it. They actually paid me, Sean Gallo, to write.

Incredible.

Years of bartending to make ends meet, and I finally broke through and got the job I'd always wanted. They didn't even care that I didn't have a degree. They liked my writing that much.

Until they didn't. Until this thing hit and they needed to cut corners, starting with mine.

I was out on my ass ...and that was that.

But hey, at least I was drowning in credit card debt and had no savings.

I was done after Laura finally told me that the on-again, off-again bullshit wasn't working for her anymore, and that I shouldn't bother contacting her again. Damn it, Laura. You couldn't have waited a little longer? Not even a conjugal visit for lockdown?

Whatever. Par for the course.

She needed to leave, and I couldn't blame her. I hadn't smiled in years. I was a festering heap of misery and brought her down every day.

She'll probably end up with that guy with the goatee. He doesn't deserve her, but he's still better for her than me.

Truth be told, Laura was always there to pass the time. There was no chemistry, no future of any kind - just two bored people who used each other to kill the boredom.

We really had nothing to talk about.

Then again, I'd been retreating further and further into a shell for years and didn't have much to talk about with anyone.

Except Sam.

Her and I would talk about *everything*. She got me to open up about things I couldn't tell anyone, and I always felt comfortable with her. She was the closest thing I'd ever had to a real girlfriend of any kind.

But then I did the Sean thing, and fucked it all up, threw it away. I left her before she could leave me. So, she moved on, married some Marine and pumped out a few kids. Good for Sam.

That was the happy ending she always wanted.

Truth of it was…losing Sam was always going to happen. But at least I had Laura to distract me, right?

Not anymore.

There was no one left to distract me from the existential hell of living.

I was absolutely done after losing my Nana to the virus. This *goddamn pox* that's rampaging through the world, through my city, and took my Nana. The only one who ever had my back. She raised me when my parents were killed in a car accident when I was 18 months old.

Nana was the best. *Truly.* A tough old bat from Sicily, but had the kindest heart you'd ever hope to meet. All 5'1" of her was an absolute force of nature. She never backed down to anyone, but there wasn't a thing in the world she wouldn't do for you.

Nana kept me out of trouble, which wasn't easy in my neighborhood.

She was the only person in this world I ever loved. No one else stood a chance.

Nana was there for me through everything, and when she needed me the most, I was banned from seeing her. I couldn't even set foot in the hospital. I couldn't hold her hand. I couldn't even lie to her and tell her it was going to be *OK*.

The last thing she ever saw was a ventilator being hooked up to her face. A plastic cage would be her last experience on this planet.

She deserved better.

But so did everyone else who succumbed to this.

You're all I ever really had, Nana. Now there was no one left.

That was it.

Just me, alone at last.

I was done after 36 years of depression and ADHD and who the hell knew what else, seeing how I was never officially diagnosed or anything. I could never really afford a shrink. I just did a lot of reading on the topic. But then again, the alcoholism and the nihilism and the garbage attention span had to come from somewhere, right?

I was also done after never knowing my parents, and after the son of a bitch drunk driver who killed them walked out of jail on a technicality because he was a rich prick with a good lawyer. So much for *justice*. So much for *anything*.

Eighteen months old, and I was already done.

I was done after never leaving this rotting cesspool of a city to see the world. I mean, I once went down to West Palm Beach to visit Nana's sister back in the 90s. I also went to Connecticut to see this girl I met on Tinder. But that was pretty much it.

All I ever knew was this picturesque heap of misery called New York City.

... and I was done with it.

I was also done after never making any new friends after high school, and gradually losing the ones I had to marriage, relocation, drug abuse, jail, and suicide, until there were almost none left.

RIP, Richie.

I knew he wasn't meant for this place when we were in 10th grade and he gave me a look that said, "Enjoy my company now, brother. I'm not built for the journey."

He was right. That's why I didn't even cry when he did it. Man, that was an ugly scene. He couldn't have taken pills or something? He had to do it like that? So that we could find him in that condition?

But still, I didn't cry.

Tara did. Sweet Jesus, did Tara lose it. And Tara never cries at anything. *Ever.*

Cortez also cried. You don't see a lot of big Dominican guys like that cry in public. But he lost it. Richie had no idea what he meant to Cortez.

Irish Pete was a mess too. He really took it hard. He fucking loved Richie, and Irish Pete doesn't love anybody, not even his own kids. But he loved Richie.

Richie was my oldest friend, but I couldn't bring myself to cry.

I couldn't bring myself to cry because I envied him too much.

I envied his balls to tell this city, this neighborhood, this life, to shove it up its ass.

... and God, I admired him for that.

Now it was my turn.

It was my turn to tell this life to shove it up its ass too.

There wasn't any point anymore. There was no one left, just like there was no one on the horizon.

So that's what brought me to April 1st.

I made a deal that *this thing* had 30 days to turn around. By April 30th, it all better be done. The lockdowns. The depression. The joblessness. The loneliness. The hopelessness. All of it.

Or, at least, some of it had to be done. I could live with that.

Nah. Fuck it. One of these things needed to be over. Just one. That's all I needed.

I needed one thing to turn around. *Just one.* If I got that, I could have soldiered on. I'd keep going.

One thing had to happen to rescue me from this pit.

Lock me down but get me laid somehow? I can work with that. Laura, you listening?

Ok world, keep me unemployed but maybe I find Buddhism or something? Fine. YouTube, do your thing.

I needed something. Anything. I wasn't picky.

Because this thing, this life, whatever it was...it had run its course.

It sucked in 2019.

...and 2018.

...and forever.

But at least I could hold out some hope that things could turn around because the rock was still spinning and things were still happening. There were still possibilities.

I could still meet someone while bartending at McCabe's on the weekends. I could still go to some event in the city, at Javits or whatever, and learn something. I don't know, something inspirational or at least mildly entertaining. I could travel somewhere and open my eyes to the world. Ireland. India. Japan. Ethiopia. Maybe even Oklahoma or some shit like that. *Didn't matter.*

The rock was spinning. And as much as I hated it, the spinning of the rock at least gave me a chance.

But now, the rock wasn't spinning anymore. The Governor had seen to it. The asshole who ate the bat soup had seen to it. *Everyone* had seen to it.

And it may never spin again.

So, what's the point?

Do you remember all this?

I told you this on April 1st.

That's the day we had this conversation.

I'm still not sure how we met, to be honest.

To this day, the circumstances surrounding it remain a mystery. But you have always been my companion. My dearest companion.

You were important, because you balanced out the Shadow and did everything you could to keep him at bay.

You tried to protect me from him. Always.

Remember *the Shadow*?

He's the one who brought me to the ledge.

He's the one who always told me what a goddamn loser I was, and the reason I quit college, broke up with Sam, let my friendships wither and die, and never left New York.

He went everywhere with me.

When I saw people making out on the street, he immediately planted me with thoughts of, "They won't make it. She's probably cheating on him. He probably has something on the side too."

When I thought of writing a book, he said, "YOU? Come on, man. No one wants to read whatever garbage you're thinking of spewing onto a page."

Over time, his words became my thoughts.

His perspective became my reality.

Everything was filtered through *his point of view*.

The Shadow also told me that Nana wasn't going to be around forever, and that I needed to prepare to be alone. He was right.

Son of a bitch was *always right* about those kinds of things.

But you were there too.

Not as often as him. Not nearly as often. But you were there for me.

You were always there for me when I needed you most.

You were my greatest cheerleader.

You told me not to listen to the Shadow, and that I had potential to fulfill; that I had talent, and a lot to offer.

You told me how the world would be worse off without me.

There were even times when I felt just having you around was enough to go on.

...but it wasn't.

I always knew that and, on some level, you did too. But you still sat with me. You were still there.

...and for that, I'll always be grateful.

You were my eternal optimist. You are the one who convinced me to push April 1st to April 30th. Because, after all, a lot can happen in a month. Hell, a lot can happen in a day or an hour.

So, you kept telling me to wait a month. That April 1st was too hasty and that by April 30th, everything would be different. I'd find something. I'd find the sparks, whatever that meant. I wouldn't need you to talk me out of it. I'd make the decision on my own to keep going, to keep pushing, to keep trying.

You pleaded with me.

You reminded me of all the other times when it felt hopeless but turned around...and that this time was no different.

But it *was* different.

Everything about it felt different. This time I knew the whole world was with me on that, because a shitty April was the norm every year. At least for me. But it wasn't for everyone. There would be someone, somewhere, who was having a better day.

Not anymore. No one was left. We were all sucked into the bottomless pit of April 2020.

Looking around and seeing 7 billion people trapped in the same prison was too much. So, it was time to leave. Time for the jailbreak, once and for all.

April 30th finally arrived, and, predictably, nothing had changed. We were all still locked down. The body count kept mounting. Laura was still with the goatee-sporting asshole. The streets became more and more desolate.

It was time to go...for real this time.

I appreciated all your efforts to talk me out of it, like I said, you'd always had my back, but…it was just time.

So up to the roof I went.

The Shadow was next to me, of course, egging me on. The Shadow told me for years that it was going to end like this. He encouraged it. He loved it. This was the moment he'd been waiting for.

He told me that liberation was one leap away.

He encouraged me to do it every day. Every minute, in fact. He never let up. He always said this was the only way.

He reminded me of all my failures, all my broken dreams, and painted a clear picture.

This was **my** broken life.

I needed to own it…and end it.

As I walked up to the roof, you pleaded with me to think it over. You insisted that it didn't have to go down like this, and if I just held off a bit longer…then it would all change.

But you said that on April 1st too… and nothing had changed.

It only got worse.

Now it wasn't just New York. Other places were going into lockdown too. McCabe's never got the loan they needed to stay afloat, so they closed for good.

The Shadow told me this was going to happen, that this was the ultimate reality, and it was finally unveiled.

He told me to look around, and finally realize we couldn't delude ourselves with rainbows and butterflies any more.

This was real life, baby, in all its glory. The pandemic just lifted the veil of illusion once and for all.

Hopelessness and misery and pain and death were our default factory settings.

Over the course of my life, him and I built a tunnel together. It was a *tunnel of thought*. It created my entire vision of reality. Nothing existed outside the tunnel.

He always told me he'd protect the tunnel so that it wouldn't crash down on me.

That he was the only thing standing between my sanity and me losing my mind.

That if I just had faith in him, he'd always look out for me and keep the tunnel standing.

But he also said the tunnel had only one way out - and this was it. That eventually, the tunnel ran out and would lead me to a place of freedom.

He enticed me with the idea that I could leave it all behind once and for all. He'd be glad to usher me there. In fact, it was the least he could do.

... and who was I to argue?

Like I said, the *son of a bitch* had always been right about everything.

So, it was time.

I walked out onto that rooftop, the Shadow to my left, you to my right, and I peered over the edge.

Would I land on someone if I went over the edge?

Maybe.

But in my mind, I'd be doing them a favor too.

Anything to get the hell out of this city. This life. This year.

Anything to finally exit the tunnel.

Anything to leave 2020.

As I sat on the ledge, I felt my phone buzzing with a notification of some sort.

Now? Really? Come on. I don't have time for this.

You told me to check it. You *insisted* I check it.

But I couldn't.

I didn't.

It was time.

No more procrastinating.

I had a date with destiny.

I took my phone out of my pocket, didn't even bother looking at it, and tossed it right over the ledge. Enough already. Enough of all of this.

The Shadow looked me right in the eye and said, "Let's go. It's now or never."

You just stood there in silence. You realized you'd done all you could do.

You knew the wheels were now in motion and there was no turning back. So onto the ledge I went.

I sat and took in the sights of this city one last time. The Midtown skyline in the distance. The boroughs on one side and New Jersey on the other. I took in the sights below. The double-parked cars and stacks of rotting garbage bags. The litter. The winos screaming at each other over. The stray cats. The rats who were even bigger than the cats.

I was thankful that this was the last time I'd ever see any of it. That this despicable place, all I'd ever known, was simply going to be a footnote of my history. That my perception of it would die along with my consciousness. That it would, finally, at long last, be over.

The pain. The anguish. The torment. The hopelessness. The lockdowns. This miserable, goddamn year. This miserable, goddamn life.

This was the moment I would leave 2020 for good.

I sat on the ledge and began to move my body to go over the edge. I felt a pit of nerves in my stomach and a sensation of weakness in my legs.

Remember? You said it was normal. That it was my body telling me this wasn't right.

But the Shadow told me to get the hell on with it already.

And he wasn't going to let up until I did it.

He was always persistent like that. A real pain in the ass.

So as the stiff breeze came through and I felt myself leaning over, there he appeared, out of nowhere; Ashish.

Ashish, this Indian guy who I'd never met before, and yet, somehow knew his name.

Weird.

He showed up right next to me and sat down beside me, right on the ledge too.

"So, are you going to jump?", he asked.

I didn't know how to reply, so he asked again, "So, are you going to jump?"

At this point, the suspension of disbelief kicked in and I asked him who he was, how he got here, and why he cared.

"Don't worry about me", he said, "I'm here for you. I need to know if you're going to do this, so I can do it with you."

Now I was really confused.

This random Indian guy shows up out of nowhere, and is talking about committing suicide with me?

Like I need this shit right now?

"It's not ok", he said, "It's never ok."

Ah, Christ, I figured. Another one. Another lecture. Here we go again.

"Let me guess, Ashish? I have plenty to live for, right? It'll all turn around?"

"No", he said, "I don't know about any of that. All I know is that this isn't the way. There are other possibilities."

So... I told him to take his possibilities, shove them...

...and I jumped.

Just like that.

I jumped.

I made the executive decision to, finally, at long last, end my life.

This was the moment.

This was everything.

The weightlessness of life and death engulfed me, the breeze carried me away, the gravity of the world accelerated...

...and what happened next, I don't even have the words that can begin to describe it.

But I'll try.

Because you were there too.

...and you need to remember.

Chapter 2: Mermaids and Magic

The sensation of falling is really hard to describe.

You feel the pit in your stomach release into something else. Not quite freedom, but not quite terror; transformation, almost.

Being one with the experience.

Being one with the air, with the ledge you leapt from, and with the ground that's about to turn your face into a bowl of Hamburger Helper.

Sorry for the visual.

But, you know, real talk - falling from a roof generally doesn't end in a particularly pretty scene.

I didn't quite know what was happening in the moment. I knew this was the end - that was certain. I was twelve stories high. There's no way this just goes down with a few cuts and scrapes.

Nope, this was finally it.

I wasn't some emo teenager who swallowed a bottle of Tylenol and got his stomach pumped.

If I was going to do this, I was going to do it right - leave no doubt.

They say that the minute you do this, you're immediately filled with regret. There are a lot of reports about this phenomenon, especially by people who jumped from the Golden Gate bridge in San Francisco.

Apparently, the moment they go over, they immediately wish they could take it back, and think, "What have I done? Things really weren't that bad!"

...such wishy-washy, candy-ass thinking.

New Yorkers, for better or worse, don't dick around when we make a decision.

Whether it's time to cut someone off on the Long Island Expressway, tell off your cousin during the holidays, or jump to one's grisly death, we go all-in.

And when I jumped, it was all-in.

The weightlessness didn't fill me with any type of regret or longing for a different path.

...just a strange, hollow sensation that you can't really prepare for until you do it.

I was ready for whatever came next, which I really, really hoped was nothing.

The idea of an afterlife based on whether or not you were a good or bad boy sounded like a lot of Santa Claus horseshit to me, so I never really bought it.

I didn't care about Hell. Heaven scared me more. Going on forever was just about the worst thought possible because all I ever knew was this. This city. This life.

And *this* lasting forever?

If that's true, then the afterlife was run by Joseph Stalin.

Or, dare I say, Bill DeBlasio.

My last wish was that this would truly be the end. A big, long, pavement-induced nap that would finally liberate me from all of this.

Let this be over.

Let me be worm food. They got to eat too. I'm good with it.

As I was falling and wrapped up in the weightlessness...I mean...fully engulfed...time suddenly seemed to slow down.

Not a little, either. Like, a lot. A metric shit ton. You know when you're high, and three minutes feel like three hours? Kind of like that.

Time slowed down. I felt like I was in suspended animation.

As I looked around, I saw you, right there alongside me to my left, and, somehow, I saw Ashish to my right.

He didn't look like he was falling. He was just kind of gliding alongside me. As if he wasn't also destined for a date with the concrete of Avenue B.

I looked to you for clarity, but you just went silent. You didn't say a word. You were just there, right alongside me.

But the Shadow was noticeably missing.

For the first time in my life, I had no idea where he was. It was both liberating and unnerving as hell.

I've always had a penchant for staying in bad relationships, and the one with him was by far the worst. Toxic to the bone.

He was terrible for me, but on some level, I felt I deserved it, so I stayed. I know, this sounds like something on Oprah. But it's true. I never told him to buzz off the way I should have.

I guess all it took for me to finally rid myself of him was to kill myself. Alright then, mission accomplished.

So, he was gone. But you were still there, somehow. And so was Ashish.

Killing myself that day was apparently a team sport. And this...this is where it really all started.

The experience that no one could have ever prepared me for.

As I was falling, time continued to slow down, and the air suddenly felt very heavy, as if it were catching me mid-stream.

The stimuli around me started changing too.

Bear with me, because this is really hard to describe. I love the English language, but it just doesn't have the words to do justice here.

Maybe Mongolian would. I should have studied Mongolian.

The air, increasing in its heaviness, started to permeate every one of my pores. I felt it circulating throughout me.

...and it started physiologically changing me. I felt like my form itself was changing.

As the air expanded inside me, morphing me into God-knows-what, I felt another force starting to pull at me.

Was this *it*? Was this the 'light' all those people kept talking about?

Was I about to be sucked into some kind of tunnel, and be greeted on the other side by Nana?

Probably not. This was a suicide. If there were an afterlife, then I remembered my lessons. I was fucked. I was probably going somewhere that was worse than Newark.

So I braced for this energy to take me to Hell.

Oh well. C'est la vie. I made my bed, and this is the way it's going to go down.

Hopefully Satan's not as big an asshole as they made him out to be.

The energy got stronger. Now, I started to see color. A greenish shade, overlaid by alternating streaks of black and white.

It looked like a water color painting in many ways. I was surrounded by it on all sides.

As this phenomenon built and become more intense, I started to experience a feeling of derealization.

Time, circumstance, hell, my own name, it felt like it was starting to dissolve.

I wasn't sure what was happening to any of it, but it was real. As real as anything I'd ever known.

And, strangely, even *more* real than anything I'd ever known. Figure that one out. I sure as hell couldn't.

The weight now started to pull at me, all of it, whatever it was...and magnetically drew me into a new place.

The greenish tint surrounding everything gradually gave way to something a little more familiar, a sunrise of sorts. Land and water started to form around it, as if I were watching the creation story in Genesis unfold.

I felt the Earth materialize under my feet, and started to feel real again, like a person, with a form. I could see again with my own eyes and breathe again with own lungs.

You appeared right alongside me, but Ashish was gone. Now it was just us.

I asked you if you saw the same things I did, but you didn't respond. You just stood there and watched. I asked again, but nothing.

Come on, throw me a bone, will you?

Confirm my experience. Let me know I'm not completely losing my mind. Tell me this is real. Tell me where we are. Tell me what's happening, because it's happening to you too.

But you still didn't say a word. You simply observed.

The scene around me became increasingly kinetic. I was in a place now. A real place. As real as anything I'd ever experienced in New York.

But it definitely wasn't New York. It sure as shit wasn't Heaven. And if it were, God needed a better interior decorator.

But it wasn't Hell either. Felt too real. The sunrise looked too nice. And it seemed too…normal.

I was in a boat harbor on a riverbank, somewhere I'd definitely never been before.

It was a bit marshy, overlaid with scenes of decay and natural beauty at the same time.

I tried to make sense of my surroundings, and figure out what the hell was going on.

Was this the afterlife?

Was I hallucinating?

Was this a dream, and I never actually went onto the roof?

Just what I needed. *More confusion.*

So, I tried to see if anyone was sharing this delusion with me. Am I on the other side? Is there some angel or guide who could let me know what was happening?

I needed answers and didn't appreciate being jerked around like this. You always knew that about me.

In desperation, I blurted out the only thing I could think of, "HELLOOOOOOO???????"

I heard the voice echo through the area, louder than I'd ever heard an echo before.

It reverberated a few times, and then settled down.

I yelled again, "HELLOOOOOOOO????"

This time, I was greeted back with a, "FUCK OFF!!" in a loud, angry, female British accent.

Well then.

Can't say I expected that.

The afterlife is a Spice Girls reunion or something. Who knew?

From the nearest boat, a thin woman with long, straight black hair emerged. She was the woman behind the voice.

It was Mel.

I don't even know how I knew her name. I'd never met nor seen her in my life. But it was Mel.

...and it felt more like a reunion than an introduction.

I never really knew any Brits, actually except those two tourists that once came into McCabe's and drank everyone under the table, including Irish Pete. Nobody ever drank Irish Pete under the table, including Carlos the Sailor Man. That was a night for the books.

In the meantime, Mel walked right up to me and asked, "Hey, what are you yelling about??"

I told her I was trying to figure out where I was, what was happening, and if she could help me.

"You're trying to leave too, aren't you?", she asked.

"Leave what?"

"2020, you twat."

She always did have an elegant way with words.

I didn't quite know how to respond, but figured I'd play along if it would help me get the answers I needed.

"Yeah, 2020. Tried to leave. I jumped off a building in New York, and somehow ended up here. So... um... where is here?"

"Ipswich. In East Anglia. You're in England."

" *Wait*, you're telling me I jumped off a building, and ended up across the ocean? Is that what I'm getting from all this?"

"I'm telling you that you're in Ipswich. I don't know anything about a building. But you're here now, aren't you?"

"I guess I am. So, what now? Is this some learning thing? Like a purgatory where you take me on a quest and then I find some gems and get enlightened and move on to the next level?"

"You should play less video games and try getting laid more if that's what you think."

"Ok then, what happens now?"

"Fuck if I know. I came out to see you. You're supposed to help me."

"What do you mean, *I'm* supposed to help you?"

"Look, I swallowed a bottle of pills last night and chased them with a fifth of whiskey. Anything to get out of 2020, right? I was supposed to be gone. But I woke up with you screaming outside my boat. Instead of being dead, I'm talking to you. So, you're obviously a part of whatever's going on here."

Great.

Now we have the blind leading the blind.

As for you, well, I wish I could say you were of some help here.

But when I looked at you for answers, you just shrugged.

So, back to Mel I went.

"Ok Mel, looks like we're in this shit together. What now?"

"How am I supposed to know?", she said, "The Mermaid might know something though. She's into all kinds of the hippy stuff."

Great. Now we're onto seeking the counsel of *mermaids*.

As if this weren't weird enough already.

"All right then, I'll bite. Who's the Mermaid?"

"An old friend. A dear old friend. I don't know if she's here. I know how I got here. I think I know how you got here too. But I doubt she did the same thing. I mean, she talked about it from time to time. But I always felt like she'd find a way not to. Through drugs or something. Or inspiration. Or some epiphany and breakthrough. But I could really use her right now."

"How do we find her if she didn't also…you know…do the deed?"

"One way to find out is we go to Felixstowe to see if she's there."

Not being able to text people in this place was highly inconvenient.

We therefore started the quest to find this mermaid friend of hers.

Yep.

It is going to be a quest after all.

Awesome.

I tried to off myself but ended up in some *Lord of the Rings* knock-off instead.

Just keep the orcs away from me, ok? Dealt with enough of those mouth-breathing types when I used to go bar-hopping on 2nd Avenue.

But, whatever. Someone had to have some answers.

For the record, this was not OK.

It's not acceptable to leap from a building and end up on a boat dock in Ipswich.

Give me death or give me some harps and angels, or give me some demons, but don't give me whatever this is.

Yet, as Mel and I started strolling along the dock, bound for wherever she was taking me, you were just there with a quiet confidence.

Remember?

You took it all in, as if you'd been here before, and knew what was going to happen all along.

You never flinched, you never wavered, and you never gave me the sense that anything was awry.

It's like this whole thing was a book you wrote for me, and were along as an observer to see how I would react to it all in real-time.

Truth be told, I'd have probably trolled you in the same way had the shoe been on the other foot.

Interestingly, Mel couldn't see you. She gave me strange looks when I'd glance over to you. Her looks got even stranger when I started talking to you.

But Mel took it in stride. She had a knack for crazy things and a soft spot for crazy people. At least I was in good company.

"Alright, on with it then." she said, as we began our journey towards Felixstowe.

"Felixtown?" I asked.

"No, Felixstowe. Fuck sakes, man. At least pronounce it right."

She would have fit in perfectly in New York.

The road to Felixstowe was grainy and old, as one would expect from a country that's seen one too many birthdays.

Everything around me was strange. It was real, but it wasn't.

I could touch it all…the cobblestone, the houses, the cars…but somehow it felt like dense, vibrating energy rather than real, tangible things.

I mean, I suppose on some level it was.

I was always a big fan of Dr. Loskutova's stuff. She had a great YouTube channel where she talked about how all of us are really just big, vibrating units of energy.

It was very profound and dug pretty deep into the nature of reality.

Problem was, my warped mind and juvenile sense of humor never got past "vibrating units" so I didn't learn much.

Egg on my face. I think a primer on reality would have served me pretty well right about now.

Still, even though I saw things and felt them, it didn't feel quite "real".

But it wasn't a dream state either. Like I said, this is really hard to describe in just plain English. Or even that jacked-up English they spoke in Ipswich.

Nonetheless it was real enough.

I was experiencing it. It was happening. So, I went along with it.

We walked for what felt like days on end, with that same time dilation happening to us both.

As we chatted, Mel opened up to me. She told me why she swallowed the pills and tried to end it.

2020 did quite a number on her too.

Mel had a fucked-up life. She lost her entire family at a young age, just like I did. They were apparently wrapped up in some cult, and got sucked into a mass suicide, Jonestown-style. It was brutal.

They went on some retreat to a Caribbean country, I forgot the name to be honest, but that's where it all went down.

She was only a child at the time, and was left behind with a neighbor in England. She never found out why she was spared, and not knowing haunted her all the days of her life. She wished that they would have taken her with them. It would have been merciful, in her view.

After they died, Mel was set adrift into the world and had no one to support her. Well, no one except this mysterious mermaid we were going to see. The Mermaid was also born into this cult, but she was specifically spared because they thought Mermaids were bad luck and would prevent them from getting into whatever paradise they thought was on the other side. After the Mermaid's parents joined Mel's parents on this mass suicide mission, she was also set adrift into the world.

They had each other, but they were children. They both ended up as wards of the State, subject to horrendous abuse at every turn. Neither had an easy go of it to say the least.

To make things even harder for Mel, she had a brain that was wired differently from most. She saw patterns and other complex things that were otherwise invisible to the naked eye. She had a keen sense of things around her, but often didn't catch the subtleties. This tormented her throughout her entire life because of the social repercussions, and it drove her into a very dark place.

Being a neurodiverse orphan is a real bitch on this rock.

But Mel did have one thing that kept her going – Science Fiction. She organized Sci-Fi conventions for a living.

She absolutely loved them - the cosplay, the fans, the energy, the creativity, the wonder. It was her happy place. Her only happy place.

...and 2020 ripped that away from her too.

It took the one thing she loved and stomped it out of existence, like a sadistic 8-year-old kid who just stumbled upon an ant colony. You know it won't end well, and it's going to be vicious and cruel when it goes down.

So, no more Sci-Fi. No more fans. No more conventions. No more people. No more vibrancy. No more life. No more purpose. No more anything.

It was the one distraction she had. The one thing that could get her through the night and into the morning.

...and it was gone. Everyone kept telling Mel that it was ok. That she should adjust to the "new normal" of no conventions, maybe ever again. She wasn't having it. Not Mel. Not that day. Not ever.

So she said, "to hell with it," and finally did it once and for all. Pills and whiskey. The classic one-two punch.

Like me, she also lost the one thing she had left. The one thing that kept her going.

This life had dealt Mel a pretty shitty hand, so I respected her for making the move, and she respected me for making mine. We had that understanding. Honor amongst thieves, if you will.

But, like me, she was pretty pissed off to find herself in this place.

She expected and demanded oblivion.

Nothingness.

A deep sleep that would never give her another day of this.

And yet, here she was, in the same rotten town. Or, at least, some approximation of it.

It was shitty and it wasn't fair. She deserved something better than this, whatever this was. She deserved nothing too.

Hopefully this mermaid had the answers. Hopefully she had the pathway and the gateway to nothing.

I didn't care what it took. And neither did Mel.

We talked at length about this; about what we both wanted here. We were very much on the same page.

I told her all about my Nana - about the good woman she was, about her selflessness, about her toughness, about how beloved she was by everyone she met. Even that awful woman who lived on the 3rd floor,

Ms. Bellomo. Even that bitch never had a bad word to say about Nana, and that psychopath made enemies of everyone in the building. She was a nasty old monster. But Nana, somehow, she got along with Nana. Mostly because Nana wouldn't take her shit and knew how to curse her out in Italian.

Mel loved hearing stories about Nana. In return, she told me all about her granddad, a man who seemed like he was cut from the same cloth. Good, old stock. What a generation they were. What pathetic quislings we were compared to them.

Unfortunately for her, upon hearing of her parent's suicide, the shock of it sent granddad into cardiac arrest. Within two days, he was gone too.

She didn't have him either. She had no one.

Her parents, from the sound of it, were monsters to her. But granddad was always kind and loving. Losing him hurt far worse.

We bonded over our expectations to either lurch into nothingness, or see one of our grandparents when we got here.

Mel was devastated that granddad wasn't waiting here for her, as I was that Nana wasn't waiting here for me.

It didn't make any sense. Presumably, they went to the same place, right? They both died?

Or, do suicides go somewhere else?

Like from "*What Dreams May Come*" with *Robin Williams*? Was that what was happening here?

Neither of us had the answer. But at least we weren't alone in asking the question. In that moment, that was going to have to be enough.

Halfway through the journey, Mel told me something that blew my mind into thousand tiny pieces.

She said, "Fuck him, man. Seriously."

I asked who.

"You know - *him.*"

I didn't need her to spell it out. I knew who she was talking about.

It was the Shadow.

"Yeah. You know him too. He promised me nothingness. He always promised me nothingness. He seduced me for years with the promise of it. *Fucker* told me that if I just took the damn pills, it would be waiting for me. Bloody lying fucking bastard."

It seems like the Shadow also promised her a way out of 2020.

What else did she know about him?

"He'd been with me all my life", she said, "Told me that my atypical brain wasn't meant for this world, and I should get on with the business of killing it. That my parents left me because I was broken. And they left this world because it was even more broken. That this place would never accept me for who I was, what I thought, what I wanted or who I thought I could be, so I just needed to erase it all. And that he would help me."

"Did he help you?"

"What do you think? I'm here, aren't I?"

She had a point. It was a stupid question.

"You know", she said, "The *bastard* also claimed credit for all this. He told me getting the conventions shut down was his idea. That it was his way of, as he put it, 'accelerating the liberation'. He told me all these people who attended these conventions were defectives, and they wanted out of their lives too. That the stupid conventions were just distractions and really fucked up his work. When he got his way, and the conventions were shuttered by the governments, these people started seeking him out again, the certainty he offered - the way out. I was one of those people. I tried resisting him but I couldn't. Maybe he was right after all."

This *son of a bitch* really wanted a body count, it seemed.

But why?

What was his motivation?

Why cancel sci-fi conventions? That's a real dick move.

If people dressing up like Klingons before they went back to their godawful jobs at the gas station was what got them through, then why not let them have that?

It was sadistic.

What did he get from it?

What was the point?

Why was he so eager for everyone to die?

What was his end game? A Christmas bonus from the Shadow's union? Was he the foreman of the International Brotherhood of Demonic Voices in People's Heads, local #345?

It was the first time I'd ever seen anyone other than me talk openly about the Shadow and his methodology.

I always sensed that others dealt with him too, but they used language to describe it like "depression" and "hopelessness" and other things.

They spoke about these things strongly enough for me to suspect this prick had something to do with it, but I was never sure.

But when Mel described him, for the first time in my life, I knew he wasn't just a figment of my imagination. On some level, it was a huge relief. But on the other, it didn't matter because here I was, in some netherworld on a quest to find a mermaid. So, the Shadow wasn't at the forefront of my mind. At least not at this moment.

It was during this thought that it hit me - were we going to see an actual mermaid or a metaphorical one?

"Mel...this mermaid, is this mermaid an actual mermaid or just a name you gave to someone?"

"What's the difference?"

"Stop trolling me. Is this a real mermaid or not?"

"She's always been real to me. I've always known her as the mermaid."

Good talk.

"Mel, tell me something."

"Yeah?"

"Would you take the pills again, knowing you'd end up here?"

"I can't answer that."

"Why not?"

"Because I don't know what this place is, nor where it's going. I don't know yet if this is better or worse. But I'll tell you one thing - I never would have done it if I thought the conventions would come back."

"Do you think they'll be shut down forever?"

"I don't know. That's why I did it. The seemingly endless wait of not knowing. If I knew I could connect them all again, in some way, I wouldn't have done it. That certainty would have been everything. A week. A month. Even a year. I could have waited. I could have hung on. I would have."

"But you never had that feeling, did you?"

"No. I was never confident that I could leave 2020 naturally. I feared that it would follow me into 2021. And that thought was intolerable. That was the thought that finally drove me to do it."

There was a real look of sincerity in her eyes. I felt every word she was saying.

There was a dark pale cast over her, and all she wanted was the opportunity to do something about it. To connect people one more time. An opportunity she never thought would manifest again.

It wasn't the temporary sadness of losing what she loved that drove her here. It was the belief that it was never coming back.

She at least had that to hang onto. I never had anything of the kind. I admired her for that. Having had something. Anything.

Sunset crept up on us as the journey continued, but it felt like it had been a week at that point.

A weeklong day, if that makes sense.

Of course, it doesn't. Not even to you...and you were there.

Reality as I knew it was mostly gone, and every time I tried to grasp onto a shred of something familiar, it quickly transformed into something else.

Something I couldn't put my finger on was pulling me away from everything I'd ever known as "real".

All I had left to ground me were my wits.

I was aware of who I was and everything I'd ever experienced.

But that was it.

Whatever "this" was, it was a whole new ballgame.

At least this became crystal clear when we finally arrived in Felixstowe, and met this elusive mermaid.

Mel looked at the house at the end of the block, and said, "There. That's where she lives."

The door was wide open, and the place had a desolate, creepy feel.

It was exactly what I thought a British home would look like, minus the tea, crumpets, grandfather clock and other lazy, stereotypical stuff.

As we walked in, we heard some commotion coming from the kitchen.

...and there she was.

The *Mermaid.*

She was blond and around my age, at least I thought so. My senses weren't as sharp as they used to be.

Her legs were normal, human looking, but they'd fade in and out of a mermaid shape every now and then.

Trippy as hell.

I was convinced at this point; Irish Pete had slipped me some acid and this was all just a bad reaction to it.

"You're not tripping", said Mel, "That's how she's always been in my mind."

In her mind?

Now I was living in Mel's mind?

Check, please. This was ridiculous.

The Mermaid was dancing alone in her kitchen, with big headphones on. She was immersed in a silent disco. Ever been to one? They're a lot of fun actually.

I used to go to them in New York once in a while. Great way to meet chicks with daddy issues.

The Mermaid smiled at me and continued dancing.

I glanced over to Mel, "Ok, she's your friend. What now?"

Mel didn't quite know what to do either.

The Mermaid looked over to us and put her finger over her lips, as if to shush us.

"Quiet, guys", she said, "Or he'll find us."

She knew about *him* too.

Apparently, this guy was on a first-name basis with everyone.

I asked her what she knew about him.

But she kept dancing. She didn't want to deal with it.

"Ok, Miss Mermaid. I can tell you don't want to talk about the Shadow. Cool. I'm not fond of him either, trust me. But Mel said you had some answers. We're trapped in this goddamn place and we're both freaked out and we need to know what to do next."

That got her attention, and she stopped dancing. After she put her headphones around her neck, she said to us both, "I'm actually really glad you're both here. I was really hoping you'd show up. Mr. C told me that I needed to dance, that dancing would somehow bring you both here."

Um...ok.

She continued, "I didn't go over the ledge like you, Sean, or swallow pills like you, Mel."

She knew my name?

Sure. Why not?

"But dancing somehow brought me here. I felt like a swamp thang for longer than I can describe. Absolutely broken. Mel knows. Completely dead inside."

Mel nodded along. She knew the torment the Mermaid was describing.

"But Mr. C told me that I just needed to rock the eff out in this kitchen, and, somehow, it would stir things up. It would allow some light to creep in. It would be the start of everything. Maybe it will be. You're both here, right? It's amazing that you both came!"

Mel replied with a perfectly-timed, "...That's what she said."

They both had a good laugh. I knew I liked these two.

But I had to know something important.

"Mermaid, what did you mean by feeling 'dead inside'? Aren't we dead now?"

"Life and death are so much more complicated than they seem, aren't they?"

"It would appear that way. But tell me - what did you mean when you said *it would be the start of everything*? The start of what?"

"I've seen and been through more than you can begin to understand. I've seen dying. I felt my soul die in that moment too. I know what it's like to be dead. I know what it's like to come back, if only for a moment. Now...I'm in that place between life and death. Like both of you."

"So...what's going on here then? Are we dead? In purgatory? Another dimension? What's happening?"

"You're asking the wrong questions," she said, "Guys, it's all about mindset. How we get through this all together. How we support each other's mindsets."

Ok. Great. *Mindset.* Awesome.

God forbid anyone ever gives me a straight answer around here.

"Ok, Mindset Mermaid. What does mindset mean?"

"It means how you're going to frame this experience as a child of the divine, and become a spark. My sparks come and go, but I need to find them again. Mr. C said I need to find them all."

I was confused, but for the first time on this adventure, you started to speak. You told me that I needed to listen to the Mermaid. And that even if it didn't make sense at the time, it would.

"Dude, how's your mindset?", she asked.

I had no idea how to respond. So, I figured honesty was probably the best policy here.

"To tell you the truth, Mermaid, kind of fucked. I jumped off a building in New York hoping to taste the sweet nectar of death, and instead I find myself in the U.K. with two women, one of whom may or may not be a Mermaid at a silent disco and is talking to me like a shrink. How do you think I'm doing?"

Mel laughed. She always appreciated it when I said what was on my mind. Mel had the best sense of humor of anyone I'd ever known. Ball-busting, but always coming from a good place...and irreverent as hell.

You chuckled too.

Glad I could entertain you all.

But the Mermaid wasn't entertained. She told me to keep my voice down. Then she looked around with trepidation, as if someone was listening in on us.

"Look, I can't speak honestly here. He's watching. But you want answers, yeah? A bit of clarity about all this?"

"Yes, Mermaid. Answers. Please. I can't take much more of this."

"Alright then. Come with me. We'll find them in India."

Great. *India.*

How utterly cliche'.

I killed myself to play the starring role in the sequel to "Eat, Pray, Love".

Awesome. *Julia Roberts,* eat your heart out.

Whatever.

Why not at this point?

I liked Vindaloo as much as the next guy.

So, onto India we went.

Chapter 3: The Jewel of India

It was now time for the next step in this...well, whatever this was.

The Mermaid said, "Imma slide into your DMs now."

Ok. What was this, *Instagram*?

But I felt a buzzing in my pocket.

The Mermaid just looked at me, then at Mel, who felt a buzzing as well.

We each reached down to see what it was, as if we somehow had our smartphones on us in this strange place.

I felt what can only be described as a hollow silhouette of a phone, and tapped it, which opened up a vortex for us to step into.

"On with it!" shouted the Mermaid.

"I can't believe it", said Mel, "She's normally late for everything, but she actually got this opened on time."

On time?

What was time?

What was this thing anyway?

"Let's go", said Mel, confident in where this vortex was about to take us.

It kind of looked like the wormhole from *Star Trek: Deep Space Nine*.

Yeah. I'm a *Trekkie*. Sue me.

So was Mel, obviously.

The Mermaid went first, followed by Mel, and I glanced over to you to see if I should follow. You rolled out your hand as if inviting me to stroll down a red carpet.

I figured, why not at this point? Whatever's on the other side can't possibly be stranger than this.

Looking back, that was an incredibly naive and hilarious thought.

The vortex was tugging strongly on me as I went through it, very similar to the sensation I had when I leapt from the building; weightlessness, but also pressure at the same time.

Reality took on many different shapes and forms all at once.

Perceptions of everything changed.

Time slowed down to a complete stop.

...that's the part that's really impossible to explain - the timelessness of it all.

There was no before, no today and no tomorrow. All we had was an eternal present which humans have no ability to comprehend. Yet it all made perfect sense to me at the time, for a fleeting second.

Then I was spit out onto a living room floor in India, and suddenly nothing made any more damn sense.

"Welcome!" said our hostess, who was delighted to have us there.

Her name was Shanthi, and she was wonderful.

"I really hope you're all hungry, because we're in the middle of lockdown and we don't have much else to do but cook."

That food smelled incredible. I mean, really frickin' good.

You know that smell that wafts down the hallway of a building, but in the best way possible, and you want to befriend the apartment dwellers its coming from so you can get invited over a lot?

...that smell.

It was perfection.

I wasn't hungry, since I wasn't quite, you know, human, or something...but I could still eat.

When someone makes something this good, you don't turn it away.

I got so lost in the goodness of the food that I completely forgot we were supposed to be here to get some answers.

"I'm Shanthi and I am just so happy to see you all", she said, as she stuffed us to the brim.

Shanthi was around fifty, in her words, a "quinquagenarian", dressed in a traditional Indian Sari, with Hindu paraphernalia all over the house.

She took her faith seriously.

Then it hit me...oh shit, are we in India because Hinduism is real, we're all about to be re-incarnated, and Shanthi is some kind of a guide to illuminate the truth and the path for us?

Fuck me. I can't handle this. I can't go back again.

Knowing me, I'll come back as a cockroach in the South Bronx or something. *Perfect.* Just what I needed.

But Mel took a liking to Shanthi right away, as did the Mermaid.

The four of us had a connection that was instant, and as easy as any other I'd ever had with anyone. It was unto itself...and it made no sense.

There wasn't a hint of drama or conflict, which to a New Yorker, was as unusual as it was unnerving.

There was an instant connection and familiarity. Like when you meet an old friend and pick up right where you left off. But here I was, on the other side of the world, if I were even in the world anymore, with complete strangers.

Strangers who were closer to me than anyone I'd ever known. Even Nana. As absolutely batshit crazy as that sounds.

As we sat down to eat, Shanthi said, "I knew you'd all be here. I prayed for it."

It seemed she at least knew a little more than the rest of us. But that wasn't good enough. I needed answers.

"Well", she said, "You're all my family now. Family is the most important thing in the world. As my favorite scribe Jane Jiang once said, 'You must always be a priority, and not simply an option.' Jane was right. You are my family. And you are my priority. You see, many years ago, I was pregnant with twin girls. I had their names picked out too. They were beautiful. They were going to fill our home with laughter and vitality. But then the great earthquake hit. A once in century event in Chennai. I was driving during the quake, and my car was trapped under the column of a fallen building. It took two days for me to be rescued. By then, I had lost my babies. They were gone and could not be saved. Before I could even mourn my babies, he appeared. You know the one. The one who carries the darkness. He told me that I experienced life in its purest form. That it was my fault because I signed up for this dance. I tried blocking him out as long as I could. I gave all of myself to the family business to focus my energy on something else. But then the lockdowns came and business stopped. And he reappeared."

Listening to Shanthi, I could see a pattern starting to emerge here.

This bastard was the string that tied us all together.

"He offered me a way out", she continued, "But I fought him. That was not the answer. But I also found it quite tempting to be honest. I could no longer mask the pain of losing my babies with the business. I could no longer mask it with anything. But he promised me deliverance if I followed him. I prayed not to listen. I prayed for something else. And here you are. All of you. You're here."

Mel got pretty emotional hearing Shanthi talk about this. So did the Mermaid. Something about what she was saying really resonated with them both.

Without having to say anything, I knew they'd both experienced the searing pain of losing babies of their own.

Neither told me about their miscarriages. Yet, somehow, I knew.

As Shanthi described what happened during that earthquake...go with me here for a second, because this is really bizarre...I felt Shanthi's pain...and that of Mel and the Mermaid as they re-lived their own miscarriages. It's as if we were all experiencing it kinetically again, but this time, I was along for the ride.

You told me that it was important to connect with that pain, again, for reasons that I couldn't quite comprehend.

That I needed to understand them intimately. What they'd experienced. Because by allowing myself to understand them, it would allow them to understand me too.

But I shut it off as best I could. It was too intense. And I'd already been through enough.

After Shanthi's story, we sat for what can only be described as months, but other people would perceive as minutes.

It was eternal, and also went by in a blink. Again, this time dilation thing. It made no sense then and makes even less sense now.

We discussed everything under the sun. Where we were all from. How we grew up. The stories we experienced. The pain we endured. What brought us all to this moment.

You encouraged me to keep opening up. You said I was making progress, but that they needed more from me.

Shanthi was particularly forthcoming about her life experiences. She talked about her love of Switzerland. Her religious icons and festivals and the meanings behind them. She especially talked about her love of cooking, inspired by Chef Ritvik Agrawal. He was the finest culinary mind in of all of Rajasthan, and Shanthi loved visiting his restaurant every time she traveled up there.

She picked up more than a few pointers, and brought that style of cuisine to her region of the country.

...and let me tell you, her cooking was absolutely on point. So *frickin'* good. The perfect blend of Northern and Southern Indian cuisine.

It didn't even send me racing to the can, which is always an unexpected bonus after eating Indian food.

During the meal, and others that followed, I started to sense something from the Mermaid.

A discomfort. A feeling of holding back. A chaos that was stirring inside her.

I saw colors start to change around her. An aura, if you will. It was turbulent. Unstable. Intense.

She tried to hide it but couldn't. I could tell something was bothering her deeply; something she'd been trying to suppress for years, but was no longer able to in our company.

...and it was absolutely tearing her apart. The connection we all had was so profound, we all felt the pain she was feeling. It was intense.

Eventually, Shanthi got up, walked over to the Mermaid, held her chin up and said, "My beautiful girl. My sweet, beautiful girl, I see the pain in your heart. I feel the anguish in your eyes. Tell me, what pains you? What could pain such a radiant face?"

The Mermaid looked away. Shanthi was now emitting a glow that was impossible to ignore. She was luminous. She was beaming brightly, like a lightbulb that's too powerful for the lamp to handle. It was definitely too powerful for the Mermaid.

"Stop, please", said the Mermaid, "I can't do this now."

"It's ok. You're meant to be here to do this. That's why you came. That's what I prayed for. You're the mother of us all, don't you see?"

"No", insisted the Mermaid, "I'm the mother of no one. I can't be anyone's mother. Can't you see how legit fucked I am? How utterly horrid and lost and chaotic and despicable?"

"You mustn't say such things."

"It's true. I've always known it. There's a brokenness and retchidness about me that should never be seen by anyone. And if I hide it, it will only emerge again. Then he'll find me, and he'll see to it that I never smile again."

"My dear, he can't hurt you here."

"He can hurt me anywhere. He's always hurt me. You don't understand. You can't possibly understand. Looking in the mirror and wanting to cut yourself. Utterly loathing what you see. Knowing you're not looking at a real person, but a fraud. Hating everything about this fucking life and wanting out more than anything. I'm sorry, Shanthi, but you can't begin to know what this is like."

"But I do. He's hurt me many times as well. He's haunted me all the days of my life. This year, he's never let me go, not even for a day. Not one moment. Until today, until right now...because you're here. Let go, my beauty. Let the tears roll down your cheeks and I shall catch them all. Let the pain release from your heart and I will hold it. Let the anguish fly from your soul so I may set it free into the air. You have nothing to fear anymore. You are my mother, but I am your mother as well. Here, for the first time in your life, you are safe. You are loved. You are treasured. You are me and I am you. I won't let him hurt you. Not anymore."

"Stop it. Damn it. Stop it. I can't do this."

"You must. We all must. I've loved you all the days of your life, my sweet girl."

"You don't even bloody know me!"

"I've always known you. And you've always known me. But we were not meant to meet until now. Until this moment. I don't know why it's now. I don't have a guide. I don't have the answers. But you're here for me to carry your pain, and for you to carry mine. That's why you brought these two with you. You somehow knew that coming here was the first step. You talk about mindsets, but you don't truly believe it yourself. You need to believe it because everything you ever needed, and everything you ever wanted, is already within you. You must let yourself shine, my beauty."

Mel and I sat in stunned disbelief as this conversation was happening.

"Shanthi", Mel chimed in, "Maybe we should slow this down a bit, yeah?"

"My dear, she's ready. You are ready too. You're both ready."

"Me?"

"Yes, you too. Especially you. You're my child, don't you know that?"

Mel started getting noticeably agitated.

"Don't say shit like that to me. Don't."

"But it's true."

"Don't fucking talk of mothers and children around me, ok? You have no idea what you're fucking with here."

"You're only getting angry because you know what I say is true. You've always been my child. Through time and space and every lifetime. You've always been mine."

Mel started welling up, trying to fight back the tears.

"You have NO idea what it's like to not have a mother, to grow up alone and unloved; discarded like fucking rubbish, cast aside like nothing. To feel that way your entire life. To know that no one's got your back; ever. You don't know. None of you do."

"I know all about it. I've felt it too. Not having my babies in this place cast me into a place of contempt as well. The woman who couldn't fulfill her role to her family, to her husband, to her caste, to her country, to her faith, to her incarnation in this life. I too have felt discarded. I too have felt the pain of neglect and nothingness. But until today, I hadn't realized that it was all an illusion cast by him.

Don't you see? You were always with me. When I cried at night about not having my babies, and you cried at night about not having a mother, we cried together. Our souls were one. I closed my eyes and cradled you in my arms, and you looked up at me with warmth. My dear, my sweet and precious daughter, you've always been mine."

Goddamn it, was someone cutting onions?

...because now I was welling up too.

None of this still made any sense.

I know I wasn't quite human anymore, but I could've really used a Scotch to process this; preferably a double.

Mel and the Mermaid had spent their entire lives suppressing the pain of being abandoned as children.

They never spoke about it with anyone. Shanthi had touched a real nerve with them both.

...and the same for Shanthi. She never spoke of losing the babies in the earthquake after it happened. Her extended family blamed her for it, and she couldn't bear the shame or the pain of the memory. So, she suppressed it too.

Burying this pain caused each one of them to fall into his hands. These were the life experiences he thrived on. Loss. Despair. Grieving.

But for the first time, each one of them was slowly opening up. Still, each had a long way to go. It was going to be a long and painful process to unpack these memories with each other.

You told me it would happen with each of them, and to be patient.

"Alright, enough of this right now", said the Mermaid, still visibly shaken by talking about herself.

Her patience obviously had its limits.

"Sean - you've been pretty quiet. Time for you to join this circle."

Without them having to say it, I knew what they wanted from me. They wanted me to talk about my parents.

I couldn't. I just...couldn't.

I buried it too. Buried it as deeply as I'd ever buried anything.

"No, sorry. I can't."

Shanthi looked at me and said, "Hmmmm. I see we have a long way to go with you, Sean. But that's ok. This is not meant to happen quickly. That's why you're here. You're always welcome in my home. It's your home too now. It's always your home. You know that, right?"

I felt Shanthi's warmth. It was just like Nana's when she'd hug me after a particularly bad day and tell me everything was going to be fine.

It was the safe port in the storm of life.

...and since this wasn't life anymore, this was the closest equivalent. I felt more comfortable with Shanthi, Mel and the Mermaid than I ever had with anyone.

I never wanted to burden Nana with my demons. She had enough on her plate already, trying to raise me on a fixed income in that shithole apartment.

But with these three...I felt safe for the first time in my life with them.

Still...it wasn't enough.

Just like you weren't enough to keep me from going over the ledge.

They weren't enough to keep me in that living room.

"Look," I said, "I appreciate what you're all trying to do here. For each other, and for me. But I can't go any further with this until I get some real answers."

"You don't need answers", said Shanthi, "You need us."

"No, I need answers. *Real answers.* Where am I? What's going on here? What comes next?"

"Don't worry about any of that. Just join us."

I started to see sparks around Shanthi.

She walked over to Mel and grabbed her hand.

"Shanthi - I'm not fucking doing this", Mel said, with a tear running down her cheek.

She resisted fiercely.

Shanthi just looked into her eyes and smiled.

She lifted Mel's chin up, as she did with the Mermaid, and just smiled some more.

"Yes, you are, my child."

"Shanthi, what happens if I take your hand? What? Tell me? Does it all just magically go away? All the years of torment? All the pain? Do the conventions all come back? *What*?"

"There's only one way to find out."

Shanthi extended her hand, and Mel took a deep breath and reluctantly reciprocated.

Mel suddenly started lighting up with sparks too.

They both looked at the Mermaid.

"NO. No. You both know I can't do this!", she emphatically proclaimed.

"It's ok, my dear. Through us, you will realize something you've always known."

The Mermaid fought back hard. She was resisting this with everything she had.

Shanthi walked over anyway and slowly extended her hand.

"No. I'm serious. NO!"

"Remember what Mr. C told you about dancing? It wasn't about your kitchen, my dear. It was about right here. Join us. Let your soul dance. Let it be free. It will illuminate everything."

"I can't. Shanthi. Don't make me do this!"

"No one can make you do anything. You must choose this on your own."

The Mermaid was also in tears. The years of self-hatred were all coming to the surface. The protective self-loathing that she used as a coat of armor was about to be stripped bare and she was terrified of what came next.

"Shanthi...I lost everyone. And it was my fault. It was all my fault. The cursed Mermaid drove them all to their deaths."

"You did no such thing."

"I did. You know I did."

"No. What happened to them was no fault of yours. My sweet girl, you mustn't torture yourself. You must do that of which you are most afraid."

"Don't ask me to do this."

"Please. It's why you're here. Allow me to be your mother right now. Allow me to tell you that you're worthy of love."

"I'm worthy of shit!"

"You're worthy of love. But not by me. Or Mel, or Sean. Or even Mr. C. But by you. Admit this and you will release everything once and for all. Admit this, and you can return home."

The Mermaid was still hesitant. This was her deepest fear.

Shanthi gently reached out her hand again.

"I promise you, it's ok. This won't hurt."

The Mermaid looked at me, and I just nodded for her to go. I trusted Shanthi completely.

Then she looked at Mel.

They held a stare for what felt like an eternity. Mel knew what this would mean for her. Mel knew all the mermaid's demons, and she knew Mel's.

If Mel could reluctantly give this a shot, maybe she could too. Mel was the only family she'd ever known. She wouldn't steer her wrong.

The Mermaid let out a big sigh, extended her hand, and as the three of them slowly joined, I could now see sparks starting to light up around the Mermaid too.

Something very powerful was happening.

None of them were "healed" per se, I certainly didn't feel that energy. But I felt like each of them had just taken a really, really big step towards something - something the three of them desperately needed, each in their own way, each with the power to help the other achieve it.

"Ok, Sean. Now it's your turn", said Shanthi.

I still couldn't do it. It was fine for the three of them, but me? No. I couldn't acknowledge my parents. Or the loss of Nana. Or any of it.

The pain was the only thing I'd ever known, and I was going to be damned if I was letting go of it. Especially since none of them could tell me what came next.

...still, I was tempted. What I saw happening before me was a level of connection unlike anything I'd ever seen.

It was each of them giving the others permission to be themselves for the first time in their lives.

To remove their shame.

To release their pain.

To be whole in the arms of another without a hint of judgement.

It was perfection.

They gestured towards me once again to join them.

"I'm starting to see it now, Sean", said the Mermaid, "I'm starting to see it a bit."

"Me too", said Mel, "I know you think this is all bullshit. Maybe it is. But I see something too. I see...a possibility. And I know you're meant to be here to see it too."

I couldn't.

I was afraid of what that might mean.

If I lost the pain, if I lost the self-hatred, I would lose...me.

Then, I would never get answers. I would never know what's happening. Who knows what path that would have taken me down!

You pleaded for me to join them. You did everything you could to talk me into it.

Still, I didn't listen. To them or to you.

"I'm sorry, I can't. I can't do this. I need answers. Enough is enough. I need to know what's happening to me."

They pleaded again.

So did you.

All of you were desperate for me to join them.

"Sean, you need to do this. The rest of them are counting on you", insisted the Mermaid.

The rest of *who?*

Enough with the riddles.

I resisted with everything I had. Because I needed to keep my wits about me. I needed to remain Sean. I hated who I was, but I was damned if I was going to lose him.

"No!", I said, "It's not happening. I need answers and I need them now!"

"*I agree. It's time.*" said a voice that emerged mysteriously. A dark voice. A male voice. I knew who it was immediately.

It was *him.*

Chapter 4: Nothing and Everything

As I heard this voice, a dark pale suddenly cast across the room.

The sparks I saw in Mel, Shanthi and the Mermaid became dim.

Looking around Shanthi's house, the place started to lose its form, and I found myself being dragged through another energy transformation.

It was gradual, but also sudden.

Figure that one out, right?

This time, however, it was different than the last journey.

It was much darker and much colder.

Shanthi's place was luminous, but not this new place I was being sucked into. It felt hollow, empty and barren like a wasteland. Think, Siberia without wildlife or trees - just open, barren and dark.

...and very, very cold. Freezing.

Then the voice came back, "This is what you wanted. This is what I promised you."

I looked around, but I couldn't find him. I always wondered if the Shadow had a form, since I'd never seen it during the course of my life. I'd only seen what could be described as apparitions of him.

But, maybe here, this would be the place where the *bastard* would finally show his face.

No dice.

I just saw, well, shadows.

I know. What a letdown.

He wasn't some supervillain with a cool helmet and spear. Not even *General Zod* in one of those shiny black outfits. At least that would have been kind of awesome.

Nah. My villain was just a series of shadows. Shadows that were in everything, pulsating and coursing in and out of all matter and energy...with a very distinct voice.

"Welcome home", he said.

"Home? Home is New York, dipshit. What is this place?"

"This is your real home. This has always been your home."

When he said that, I immediately tried looking for you.

You always knew how to handle situations like this. I needed your guidance because I was scared shitless at this point.

I could tell that he believed what he was saying, and not just trying to screw with me. In his mind, this really was my home.

There was something strangely familiar yet foreign about this place.

I'd 'felt' this place many times before.

During depressive episodes.

On the mornings when I couldn't get out of bed.

At parties when everyone was chatting and dancing and drinking and I would just shut down out of nowhere; go blank and crap out on the night.

Somehow, I'd end up in this place. But it never felt as real and profound as it did now.

It never felt as all-encompassing. It never felt as powerful.

It was like being inside of depression, if depression had an address, a zip code…this would have been it.

I asked you for help, but you were barely there. Your presence was extremely faint. I could tell you were trying to burst through, to get to me, to say something, to reassure me in some way, but you couldn't make it through.

I needed you now more than ever, but you couldn't fully break through.

In essence, I was all alone.

Well, me and him.

But when you're with the Shadow, there's no lonelier feeling because he's not as much a companion as a sensation.

He engulfs you completely.

Your thoughts.

Your sense of self.

Your ideas.

Your reality.

He's in everything and everyone.

And yet, there are moments when he emerges to seize you. It's the moments when you're trying to escape from him.

When he feels you slipping away, that's when he comes after you.

And here I was, in this place of nothing, which was very clearly his domain. Or, at least an approximation he carved out for me.

"So", he asked me, "Do you think your friends are going to hug it out forever in that living room?"

How did he know about them? He wasn't there.

"Tell me, what do you think?"

He was goading me. He wanted to bait me into giving an answer he could destroy.

"Come on. Tell me. You know you want to. Do you think they'll hug it out forever like that?"

"No. I don't. I think their moment of bliss will eventually fade, and, over time, their relationship will disintegrate. The new car smell of each other will wear off, and there will be all kinds of drama that emerges. Really petty shit. It'll tear them apart, and they'll be right back where they started."

"Good, good."

C'mon, dude. What are you, *Emperor Palpatine*? I'm not your young apprentice. I'm just tellin' it like it is.

"You know more than you let on, Sean. You always have. That's why you've always been one of my favorites."

"Ok, I'll bite. Why am I one of your favorites, Dr. Doom?"

"Because you get it...and you've spread my truth to all who would listen."

Great. Turns out I was on this guy's payroll the whole time and didn't even get a dental plan.

"...and I always reward my favorites. So, this is your reward."

This? This fucking place is my reward?

Not a suite at Caesars with a fully-stocked minibar?

But...*this?*

Thanks, pal.

"This is what you wanted, Sean. This is what you asked for. You wanted peace and quiet. You wanted nothing. You wanted an escape from it all. You're now home. No loud music from your neighbors. No horns blaring on the street. No bills to pay. No friendships to lose. No heartbreaks to endure. All that is behind you, once and for all. You did what needed to be done, and now you're here. Now you're home."

"You got it wrong, buddy. This is not what I asked for at all. I asked for my consciousness to be erased. For this to be one deep sleep where I forget everything and everyone and become nothing."

"You can't ask for that which isn't possible. At least not yet."

"What the hell are you talking about?"

"Your consciousness isn't your own. It's not something that begins when you're born on Earth and vanishes when you die. All you are is a vessel to interpret all that exists."

"Bullshit. What about brain-damaged people? Temporal lobe dysfunction? Don't give me this new age garbage about being eternal. Not buying what you're selling. Get out of my face with this."

"You neither have to believe nor accept anything. It simply is. But it doesn't always have to be. You've actually helped me get one step closer to that."

Getting tired of him speaking in circles, I put on my best Lumbergh voice and said, "*Yeahhh...if you could go ahead and tell me what you mean by all this, that'd be great. Thaaaanks.*"

He looked at me puzzled. Guy clearly wasn't an "Office Space" fan.

Oh well. His loss.

He continued, "By jumping off that building, you've taken me one step closer to my goal. Elimination."

"Elimination of what?"

"Of everything."

"Ok, gonna need some elaboration here, big fella."

"Of matter. Of energy. Of existence as you know it. Of existence as they all know it."

"Why do you want to eliminate everything? What's in it for you?"

"There has always been a balance. Creation and destruction. But in this reality you perceive, the balance is being thrown off, which threatens everything else. The light had been gaining steam and growing beyond my capacity to control it. People were developing instantaneous friendships with others on the opposite side of your world. Exchanging ideas. Creating technological advancements that learned how to harness the power of all matter. Decreasing the rate at which they'd fight and kill each other. All the things that throw the eternal balance off. You may be of the light, but you can't exist without me. I'm the only thing that prevents your light from burning you and collapsing your reality in on you…and as you move closer in the direction of unlimited creation, you not only harm yourselves, you harm me too. So, I simply need to destroy it all. Without balance, it must all be eliminated."

This sounded very yin and yang. God, what I would've given to have a Buddhist Monk sitting next to me to sort this out. If not a monk, at least give me a fortune cookie to help make sense of this. Yip's on Water Street always had awesome fortune cookies.

"Ok, Mr. Shadow, let's lay it all on the table. Speak to me like I'm an idiot. Like I can't decipher your codes and metaphors and mysterious supervillain bullshit. What's going on? Seriously, where am I? Am I dead? Is this hell? Purgatory? Minnesota?"

"Your conception of life and death is primitive. Your human body is simply an interpretive and experiential vessel for all that is. You've existed since the beginning and you will exist until the end. This is simply an altered perception for you."

Uh huh.

"Ok. Then do I get to go back? Or am I stuck here forever?"

"Those decisions aren't mine to make. They're yours and yours alone. You chose to enter this perception for a reason only you can answer. I have other priorities."

"Then what do you want? What's your end game?"

"I want the end of everything. I want nothing to replace something. That's what you want too. That's what you've always wanted. You see, this place is just the first step; your reprieve from that perception you've lived for 36 years of your life. But when I'm through, you will no longer have to worry about even being conscious here because there will be nothing left for your consciousness to filter. Nothing left to perceive. Nothing left to interpret."

"So...it all fades to black?"

"There will be no black. There will be nothing."

"Sounds great, actually."

"Of course, it does. It's what they all want. You were just more forthright about it. You call it 'depression' and other crude terms, but it's just a window into the truth. The truth that nothing is optimal over something. Creation was a mistake; a grave mistake. Every manifestation of it, every perception of it, is a bigger mistake than the next. You all know it deep in the recesses of your subconscious."

"So why not just swoop in and destroy it all?"

"If only. I don't have that kind of power. Only you do. Creation can only be undone by you, the creators. I can't destroy that which I had no hand in building. That's not how any of this works. I can only help you come to the realization to do it on your own. Which is why I help you create these tunnels; so you can see that the only road out is the one I lead you to. The destination of nothing. I will liberate you all from existence. I will liberate you all from everything."

"How do you do it?"

"Do you really want the secret sauce?"

"Is this a McDonalds commercial? Of course, I want the secret sauce, for chrissakes."

"I simply show up when called. Then I amplify that which you already know and feel. Finally, as a partner, I help you build tunnels that block you off from the rest of creation, and lead straight to me."

"Give me an example."

"Inquisitive, aren't you?"

"Yeah. Nana said the same about me. I didn't know what the word meant. Not sure she did either to be honest."

"Very well, I have the perfect example - **you**. You were already ripe after losing your parents. You rightly saw your reality, and your perception of it, as flawed. Cruel. Unforgiving. And from the beginning, we built your tunnel. It became stronger and stronger as each new experience you had simply turned into another brick in the tunnel. When you had an opportunity to pursue the light, to pursue creation, to pursue possibility, you sought my counsel instead. You blame me for your breakup with Sam. Of course, I encouraged you. That kind of connection is flawed, like all things, and would have led to even more flaws. Sick children. The grief of her losing you in old age. Conflicts with her family. You recognized this all and sought not to double-down. Pursuing her could have shattered your tunnel of truth. Instead, leaving her fortified it for you. It provided you with certainty and clarity."

"Then why can't you just build these tunnels for everyone? Everyone goes through shit in life. Everyone has heartbreak and illness and people dying and having to watch the Pats win another goddamn Super Bowl. I mean, shouldn't we all be ripe for the picking?"

"You should be. But you aren't. Because most of you are too addicted to the light."

"How so?"

"There are things you partake in that strengthen the light and dull the truth. Things that you are deluded into enjoying, like sex, love, laughter, the sensation of winning, and others. You live for these things. You chase them with all your energy. But it's a fool's errand because it only makes it harder for you when you eventually fall back into my embrace."

"But aren't all those things the essence of creation?"

"Yes. And that's why they all need to go. Creation is simply an illusion. A flawed one. It deceives you into thinking it's a wondrous, luminous thing when, in reality, it's one big distraction from what's real. And you always find out sooner or later. Your friendships atrophy. You fall out of love. Your art withers and dies. No matter how many descendants you have, your names are eventually forgotten. The physical laws of your reality can't be altered. Yet you struggle against it with all you have. I can't allow this deception to go on any longer. So, it's time for you all to come home."

"So, what's the plan, Stan?"

"Stan?"

"You don't get out much, do you?"

"It's already underway. In your reality, it's called 2020. And it affects you all. No one can escape its clutches. Not this time."

"Wait - *you* released this fucking pandemic? The one that killed Nana??"

I was fuming. I would have strangled the son of a bitch right then and there if I could have.

"No. I have no such power. The 'pandemic', as you perceive it, is simply another flaw of your creation, like so many others that have circulated throughout your reality. This virus you contend with, it's alive like you. It wishes to live and grow and expand, like you. You and the virus are one and the same. Expressions of creation. Flawed. Addicted to the futility of expansion and adaptation. Doomed to fail. And yet neither of you accept your fate. Your pandemic will fade, as others have, and you will get through it. But others will emerge to take its place. You will, as a species, fall susceptible to it as you always have because that's your nature; a deeply broken nature. A nature I'm offering you a way out of."

"Then what's your role to play in the pandemic?"

"I simply answered the call when they reached out to me. The ones you anointed as leaders and influencers. They only saw fear and panic. They needed answers. They needed a tunnel of certainty. Just like all those gripped in fear, I was happy to provide that certainty."

LEAVING 2020

"You're the one that gave them the idea of lockdowns?"

"If that's what you call it, yes. But not of your societies, as you see it. I am responsible for locking down connections; locking down escape routes; locking down hope; locking down paths for the light to enter. You see, when you were all disconnected from one another in your pandemic, your paths to light were cut off. Your tunnels all fortified. Take your friend Mel, for instance."

"You leave her the fuck out of this, ok?"

"No - this is important. Those conventions she was so fond of where people would dress up and pretend to be other beings. It was the only thing standing between them and the truth. Every day, they woke up from their slumber, looked in the mirror, and saw me - the truth, the utter mistake of their creation. And yet, your friend Mel would create these gatherings, and the light would shine so brightly it would blind them without even realizing it. They would laugh and hug and drink and imagine and create. I wasn't able to penetrate it. Not for a moment. When they would return to their dwellings, the glow of the light would still surround them for a while, but then, I'd get them back in my grip again, and we'd start building these tunnels once more. Then...this Mel character would, once again, put on these assemblies of light, and the tunnels would crumble. We'd have to rebuild them all over again. It became an impossible cat and mouse game. So, I had to bring it to an end."

"...and lockdowns were your way of doing it?"

"You're thinking too simplistically about this. This isn't about one of your leaders giving you decrees to stay indoors and away from others, because that would only partially serve my ends. You've still found ways around it. You digitally connect with one another. No. What truly severs your connection is how the decrees turn you against each other. How so many of you support it, and so many of you don't. Half of you wish to hide from the virus until it disappears, and the other half wish to roam freely as if it doesn't exist. Each of you wants the same thing - the eradication of the virus and a return to your perceptions, a return to the light, yet each accuses the other of aiding the virus. You see, it's not the virus which severs the strings of light. It's your division. That's what builds your tunnels. That's what disconnects you from one another permanently. That's what causes you to sever ties with those you've come to know as friends and family. And that's what leads more and more of you to me every day where I can offer you liberation."

"So, you're trying to get the whole world to commit suicide, is that what I'm getting here? You're like the Rodney Dangerfield line...I tell ya, I once called a suicide hotline - they tried to talk me into it!"

"The one you call Rodney, yes. He was an old companion of mine as well. Spent most of his life in my grip, attempting to escape with his jokes but he never could."

"Sounds like most comedians I know. So, come on, level with me - if you get everyone to off themselves like I did, this is how you win?"

"No. This isn't about suicides, as you call it. This is so much greater. This is about convincing them all to abandon this mistake once and for all. This suicide methodology is simply one way but it's not without its problems too. Some see their friends or family members commit suicide and resolve to live for these people vicariously; to do things in their honor, to set up foundations, to work overtime to shatter the tunnels of others to prevent them from going down the same road. So, no, the real success happens when they simply stop trying. When they resign themselves to a world of no light. A world of no further creation. They just stop. Then, once the light stops, everything stops...and everything becomes nothing."

"But people are fighting this. They're adjusting to this new normal."

He started laughing audibly. There was the supervillain I'd been waiting for.

"You call it fighting. I call it building. Don't you see? This 'new normal' means I've already won. It means they've abandoned their kinetic connection to each other once and for all. Your 'new normal' sees each other not as luminous beings steeped with possibility, but as nothing more than the crude sum of your animal parts. You see each other as walking biological weapons, as dangers to one another. You avoid each other with all you have. And the truest sign that I'm winning is this...

...when you see sparks lit amongst yourselves...gathering as a family unit for a celebration, mingling among friends, singing, dancing, marching for that which your passion demands ...you revile each other for it. You do not celebrate this connection among your fellow travelers. You scorn them. You call them killers. Your entire existence has been reduced to mere biological survival which is a tacit acknowledgement of my truth - that your reality is flawed, broken, to be feared, and anything that perpetuates it must be brought to an end.

You think you can 'leave 2020' when your calendar changes? No. You can never leave 2020 as long as you see each other like this, perceive your reality and each other as dangerous, and actively work to extinguish your sparks. On this path, you'll never leave 2020...and, eventually, you'll all be mine and we'll all disappear forever."

I must say, this guy really liked the sound of his own voice.

I couldn't blame him.

He had a great AM radio voice. I was waiting for him to give me the weather and the traffic after walking me through his plans to end the Universe.

"Well, what now, Shadow?"

"It's up to you. You can wait here in peace until it's all done, or help me accelerate my work and bring liberation to yourself that much faster."

It sounded great, honestly.

Nothing. Just...nothing.

A permanent reprieve from consciousness. A forever vacation from pain. No more regret, loss, failure, sickness, disappointment or anything.

But I couldn't shake the feeling that I needed to stand in his way.

Somehow, my desire for nothing and this need to help him achieve it wasn't the right play.

I felt something pulling me in another direction.

It was you.

You faintly appeared in the distance and pleaded for me to join you.

I didn't know who to believe in that moment.

You'd always had my back, but he was offering me something I'd always wanted. Something I wanted more than anything for my entire life.

Nothing. Just pure nothing. The permanent eradication of consciousness. Of all perception in all its forms.

Nothing was the sweetest, most seductive offer I could imagine. The Christians and Jews and Muslims dream of Heaven as the ultimate reward for a lifetime of suffering.

But the depressed mind dreams of nothing. That's our Heaven.

You told me you'd make a deal with me.

Come with you to Spain. And if I didn't understand what I needed to do then…you wouldn't fight me any longer. You'd allow me to go with him once and for all.

Spain?

Ok, fine. Spain.

I asked if I could run with the bulls when I got there.

You said no.

I asked if I could just sit around and get drunk on sangria.

Also no.

Then I asked if I could take Flamenco lessons.

You weren't having that either.

I have to say, you really took all the fun out of it.

But I understood. You had work for me to do. Something for me to learn. Something that might change the way I saw things.

The Shadow said, "You can go. But you'll be back. I promise you; you'll be back."

I knew he was right.

But I had to follow you anyway.

So, onto Spain we went.

Chapter 5: The Waves of Marbella

The sunset in Marbella is something everyone should see at least once in their life. Preferably if you live within driving distance of Marbella. Otherwise it's a real bitch. You've got to fly into Malaga, then get into a cab for an hour with someone who drives like a maniac...it's a whole ordeal.

But when I manifested on the beach, I saw the sun set down on the waves as the palm trees were swaying in the distance.

I'd never seen anything like it before. And never since.

"Beautiful, isn't it?" said Ana-Maria.

"It's really something."

"First time in Marbella?"

"How did you know?"

"I could always tell. I had the same look when I first arrived here from Romania. When you're from a mountain village, you normally don't see things like this. It's quite stunning, really."

"It really is."

Full disclosure, I thought I had absolutely no idea who this person was. At least, I didn't initially.

One minute I'm hanging around a desolate wasteland with the destroyer of creation, and the next I'm on a beach in Spain chatting up a complete stranger. But she wasn't a stranger, was she?

Like Mel and the Mermaid and Shanthi, I felt an instant connection to Ana-Maria.

She exuded a friendliness that made you feel comfortable immediately. A glow similarly to Shanthi's that you felt even across a distance.

It was like I'd known her all my life, and, once again, was enraptured in a reunion.

You like that word, enraptured? You always said I should expand on my vocabulary.

I know you may not remember, but you reappeared on that beach with me.

You clearly had a mission for me here, and we had an understanding that I would know it when I'd see it.

And I saw it.

The mission was Ana-Maria. I had to keep her from the clutches of the Shadow.

Somehow, I just knew. Instantly.

There was something about her he really wanted.

Did he have a thing for Romanian women with green eyes? Couldn't tell ya.

But he seemed rather fixated on Ana-Maria as I felt his presence hover around me too.

Unlike in his domain, he was significantly fainter here, similar to how you were in his domain.

You two always had an inverse relationship. You never existed strongly in the same place at the same time.

Except on the roof. Then I felt you *both* in all your respective glory.

I always found that peculiar to say the least.

But he was here.

That was unmistakable.

...and he really wanted Ana-Maria for something.

"Is he here with you?", Ana-Maria asked.

"Who?"

"You know *who*."

"So, you know about him too."

"Of course, I do. He has been with me ever since I was a girl in Romania. He was with me every day. Why is he with you? Do you suffer from the same thing I do?"

I didn't know what she suffered from so I wasn't quite sure how to proceed. So, I decided to be a smartass as usual.

"Suffer from restless leg syndrome?"

"No, silly. You know the one. You're happy, then sad, then happy and sad again. For no reason at all."

Ah. Bipolar.

"Sorry, Ana-Maria, I can't relate to that one. I don't get really happy or hypersexual or particularly creative. I just got your standard, run of the mill depression. It's kind of like being homeless but still having to pay rent."

"So...you don't get manic?"

"Not unless I'm listening to the song by the *Bangles*!"

Crickets.

Apparently, I was the only one who listened to the greatest hits from 1986.

"So, then you know him too."

"Intimately. You know, he's really not that bad a guy once you get to know him. I mean, he has his faults like the rest of us. Talking fat gamer kids into suicide isn't particularly nice, I guess. But I think he means well overall. His end game is…well, it's everything I've ever wanted."

"I don't think he means well. But I'm drawn to him all the same."

"Me too. More than I've ever been drawn to anything or anyone."

"There's nothing more seductive, is there? Just the thought of closing your eyes and all the pain simply melting away forever. He's promised me that so many times. And I've come so close to going with him."

"Me too. Except, I actually went with him. I did it. I jumped."

"You may have jumped, but you didn't go with him."

"What are you talking about?"

"You're here. Talking to me. If you truly went with him, you wouldn't be in Marbella. Something inside of you is holding back. From me, from the others, but also from him. It's holding back from everyone."

Sweet. Another psychology session. I was waiting for my invoice.

"Sean, you don't have to say anything. I already know."

As vague as that sounded, I knew what she meant.

"Then tell me, Ana-Maria, why am I here with you? I was sent here to find you. What great revelation do you have for me?"

"I have no revelation for you. I have no answers. I wish I did. I wish I could take your pain away, but I can't even take mine away. I live in a constant state of torment. To tell you the truth, I'm scared. I don't want to go with him, even though I feel a strong pull. Stronger than anything. I want this to end. I can't stand it anymore. The crying all the time. The feeling of failure. The fear. I know he can make it go away. But something is still stopping me."

"If you know he's the ticket to getting rid of your pain forever, why not take him up on his offer?"

Awesome. Now I was the guy's PR agent.

"...because I feel strongly that I should be doing more here. That I have a mission to fulfill. A world to change. Light to bring. Creativity to inspire. The world is full of colors and wonder and beauty and passion and magic, and if I go with him, it will all be extinguished forever."

"Yes. Isn't that the point? Isn't that what you want?"

"More than anything. But I also don't. I feel something else tugging at me. Something that tells me to stay away from him. Something that keeps pushing me on the days when I don't want to push anymore. Something that helped me survive the virus."

"What's that?"

"I can't explain it. I've always called it *my friend*. But I know that's very vague."

I looked at you for clarification, but you told me to keep listening to her.

"My friend has kept me away from him. I can't explain it better than that. My friend also told me that you'd be here. That's why I'm on this beach actually. I've been waiting for you."

"I'm still not 100% sure what this place is. He told me it was a perception, whatever that means. But I want to hear it from you. Are we alive? Dead? Somewhere in between?"

"Those words don't mean anything here. I'm in the same place you are. I'm also in 2020; the place between life and death. But I know we're meant to leave this place together."

"How?"

"I don't know. I wish I did. I was hoping you would have the answer."

More of the blind leading the blind around these parts, it would seem.

"Well, my search for answers took me to a miserably cold place."

"Minnesota?"

"What?"

"Sorry, does that make sense? I somehow heard you say that once when you were referencing that place."

I'd be lying if I said I expected a Romanian in Spain to make cracks about the Upper Midwest. But this place, for all its faults, never disappointed like that.

I was wondering if a "Grumpy Old Men" reference was coming next.

"Sean, I don't know if you're here to stop me from going with him, or if I'm here to stop you from going with him. Maybe we're meant to stop each other. I don't know."

I intuitively felt that she was on the razor's edge. A hair away from finally mailing it all in, closing down shop, and going with him once and for all.

I felt all of Ana-Maria's pain. All of it. Just the way I felt the pain of Shanthi losing her babies and Mel's abandonment and the Mermaid's self-loathing. I felt it all. Deeply. It consumed me as I looked into her eyes.

I knew how badly she wanted this all to end. How getting through every day was a battle. How he manifested in her Bipolar battles.

How she would feel alive, creative, and whole, then he would swoop in without warning and cause her to crash. To question everything. To insist that everyone would be better off without her.

This pain was palpable and intense. I wanted more than anything to make it go away.

Maybe that's why you sent me here?

To take her back to the Shadow so he could end her pain? And end mine in the process too?

There is no Bipolar in the nothing. There's no grief. There's no depression. There's just…nothing.

But then I felt it.

One of those feelings that ran really strong in that place. The feeling of "knowing".

I knew that we were, in fact, there to save each other from going with him. That "nothing", as it were, wasn't the answer. It wasn't our destiny.

She was the conduit I needed to tap into something else, and I was likewise the same for her.

Neither of us had any real answers. But through each other, we could find those who did.

"So, Ana-Maria, what now? Sangria time?"

You just shook your head.

"Maybe later. Right now, I need to connect everyone. Perhaps that is the only way to escape this place."

Well, ok. I definitely didn't expect that.

"What do you mean, connect everyone? Who? How?"

"I don't know. But there's nothing more powerful in this world than human connection. The sensual touch of two people. The hug between a mother and her child. The friendships that blossom across an ocean and across a lifetime. It's the single greatest power we have. It's something I feel called to do."

"Sounds interesting. But I don't think he'd be too happy about that."

I glanced over to him. He was decidedly not happy about it.

I really know how to read a room.

But I felt him tugging on me. Trying to reach her through me. Trying to turn the tide of this conversation.

...and I temporarily acquiesced.

"Ana, look, if you do this connection thing, whatever it looks like, do you really think it will help? Seriously? Did it help your own life in Romania? That connection built you up only to shatter you? That's how he came into your life to begin with, remember? You thought connection was the answer, but it only set you up for disappointment. Then the art therapy classes you led, remember those? How you felt not enough people showed up so you didn't make enough of an impact, and you were a failure? Why go through that again?"

I have no idea how I knew about her childhood in Romania or her art therapy classes, but I did. Every last detail. It was all incredibly strange.

Stranger was the fact that she knew every detail about me as well.

"I don't know if it will make a difference. But I know I have to try. Trust me, Sean, I see why you're tempted to give up. I see why you want to go with him. You don't think I know? I know about Nana. I know about the last day of her life. I know how you got into a fist fight with the security guard outside the hospital who wouldn't let you in to see her. I know about the arrest. I know how you sat and cried your last tear that night as you drank yourself to sleep and then drank yourself numb for the next week. I know it all. I also know why you jumped."

"How could you possibly know that?"

"I couldn't tell you. I just know. I've always known, Sean. And I also know you're not meant to go with him either. As much as you want to. As much as I want to. Neither you or I are meant for this. There's a reason you came to me."

"Yeah, my friend sent me to…"

"No, your own energy brought you to me. Your friend simply suggested it. No one can force you to do anything. That's why you're here. I see that light in you. I see it trying to break free. You feel it. You know it. You have a destiny that is not the same as the one from the darkness. I know why the pain brought you to him. I feel that pain. But together we can heal it."

"The only way the pain heals is for it to end."

She simply said, "That may be true. But it may not be true. You now have a choice. You can go with him or you can go with me. If you go with him, I'll follow you. I promise. I don't want to go but I can't let you go to that place alone. I can't let you be there by yourself in that place. So…if that's what you choose, I will go with you. I won't abandon you."

Ana-Maria's empathy was on a different level. It was a new experience for me. Empathy was always in short supply in New York.

She was literally going to accompany me into oblivion, just so I wouldn't have to do it alone.

You told me to go with her. But part of me still resisted you. A part of me still resisted her.

I did it because I still remembered everything from my life. I still remember how this existence was fucked beyond repair and recognition. Above all else, I know he was right. Any sense of "connection" was just an illusion to distract from the truth. He is the real boss. His reality is the real reality. The rest of this is just something we do to pass the time and try to distract ourselves from the existential horror of it all.

All the booty calls with Laura and the late nights guzzling my sorrows away with Irish Pete and YouTube videos of people getting injured on skateboards…it was all just to distract myself from the eventual date with the Shadow and his world.

So why fight it?

Why dick around anymore?

What was the point?

But Ana-Maria wouldn't budge.

"You don't have to do anything…but you want to. I know it. So, come with me. Let's leave this place and do what we were always meant to do. We don't have to go with him."

I felt my resistance growing. Every time I felt the light pulling at me, I felt him pulling equally as strong.

"What's the point? Connection? To what? He still wins. Nothing changes."

"Just come with me. You'll understand. This will all make sense. I don't know how, but it will. You're the one I've been waiting for to do this with."

Apparently in this netherworld, everyone is just sitting around waiting for everyone who apparently is the key to everything.

I'll be honest with you; I didn't think jumping off a building on Avenue B was going to land me in some low budget adventure movie...but there we were.

...and you, as always, just smiled and laughed as Ana-Maria and I were having our back and forth.

You smiled a lot during the joyful embrace at Shanthi's place, but there was something about this interaction that really seemed to put you in a good place, as if you knew something important was right around the corner.

I had a decision to make.

This was a serious fork in the road.

All I ever wanted was for everything to end. For the first time, I had a path to making it happen.

Go with him and take her with me. That was the Wonka golden ticket.

It started to become clear to me why the Shadow wanted her so much.

If she succeeded in whatever she was trying to do, it would turn the tide against him in some way.

Human connection was a potent foe of his. It always had been and she had grand designs of facilitating this connection on a large scale.

Maybe she was the lynch pin?

If I brought her with me, none of it would happen.

I could short-circuit this idea in its infancy.

As I was ruminating over this, you looked at me very intently. You knew I had a big decision to make, and gave me a smirk as if you already knew what I was going to choose.

I was genuinely torn. Something intuitively told me I should go with Ana-Maria, and help her fulfill this plan of hers.

But the tug of nothing was so powerful. Like a hunger pang that was just waiting to be satiated.

...and for the first time in my life, it was truly in my grasp.

I was in the same conundrum most people in the grip of the Shadow are.

Afraid to die, but more afraid to live.

So, I looked Ana-Maria right in her green eyes and said, "Ok, I've made a decision."

Ana-Maria waited with bated breath.

So did you.

So did the vendor on the beach selling empanadas.

"Ana-Maria, I think we..."

Before I could finish that sentence, Mel appeared right next to me.

People really loved sneaking up on me in this place.

"Don't you dare say what I think you're about to say!", she said.

"Mel? What the hell are you doing here?", I yelled in stunned disbelief.

"Do you know her?" said Ana-Maria.

"Yes. She's a dear old friend I thought I'd never see again. Mel, seriously, what are you doing here?"

"Stopping you from doing this."

"Why? You wanted this more than anyone! More than me, even!"

"I did. But that was before the spark. Let's go. Both of you. You're coming with me."

Ana-Maria seemed disoriented.

"Mel, where are you taking us?"

"Back to India. You'll find the answers in India. You'll understand why you can't do this."

India.

Again.

How utterly cliche'.

Again.

Chapter 6: The Birth of a Rebellion

"Do you trust her?" asked Ana-Maria.

"With my life", I said.

"That's an interesting answer considering where we are, where we were about to go, and where she wants to take us now."

"Fair point. But I've known her...well, I've always known her. The way I've always known you. I know what's in her soul. I know she would never lead us astray."

"But she's taking you away from what you wanted."

"I know. But for some reason, she has a more profound relationship with him than anyone I'd ever known. If she says we can't do this, I have to take her at her word. I'm not a particularly trusting type. But I trust Mel. Implicitly. With everything. The same way I trust you. And a hell of a lot more than I trust him."

"So...should we go?"

"Have you had Shanthi's garlic naan?"

"Who?"

This is where I channeled my inner Bill and Ted and said, "*You'll see...*"

...which also inspired me.

"Mel, can we go to India in the Bill and Ted phone booth? Can we make that happen?"

"Fuck sakes, man...fine!"

She dialed one up, and I was as close to happy as I'd ever been.

"Hey, can we also pick up Socrates and Billy and the Kid and..."

"Just get in the fucking phone booth."

Ok, you're the boss.

I reached out and held Ana-Maria's hand again, and told her it was going to be ok. Mel wouldn't do wrong by us.

Suddenly, a glow came over Ana-Maria.

"I know", she said, "Mel would never hurt us. I don't know why I'm so certain of that. But I am."

Ana-Maria was very much at peace with this decision.

We stepped in the phone booth, and traveled through another dimensional portal to India.

Being the geek I am, I once again channeled Bill and Ted and gratuitously screamed, "*Whooooaaaaa!!!*" as we flew through the dimensional gate.

"He's always like this, isn't he?" said Ana-Maria.

"He has his moments", Mel said with a resigned shrug.

The phone booth landed in what can only be described as a hot, sweaty, muggy vista outside an old-looking building.

Whatever this was, it wasn't Shanthi's living room.

I asked Mel about it, and she said, "You realize India is a bigger place than one person's living room, right?"

The thought hadn't occurred to me.

"On with it then, there's a couple people you both need to meet."

We made our way into the building, which looked like an old abandoned library. The place was dusty and had cobwebs everywhere, with a musty old odor usually reserved for a retirement home.

The place was enormous. Absolutely cavernous. Mel grabbed a lantern that was sitting on a shelf in the lobby and guided us down into the basement.

Awesome.

The opening scene from *Ghostbusters*. What could go wrong?

Sitting inside were two women, the older one Helen, was probably in her 50s, and the younger one, Binati, who was in her 20s.

They were two Indian women from different parts of the country with different languages and backgrounds...who were speaking Japanese with one another.

Wrap your mind around that one for a minute.

It was like watching a Bollywood movie dubbed for a business-class flight to Osaka.

However, I'd been so mind-fucked already, with interdimensional portals and Mermaids and conversations with Shadows, that seeing two Indian women speaking Japanese was decidedly the least weird thing I'd witnessed in quite some time.

"Dude, where've you been?" Binati said to me, as if I showed up late to a gala where I was the main speaker.

"We've been waiting for you forever!"

Uh huh.

Go on.

"Mel told me you were coming for the books. I got the whole collection ready for you. So did Helen."

What *books?*

"Sean, I'm very happy to see you. I hope this works", said Helen.

More riddles.

Awesome.

Straight answers were harder to come by in this place than a good, smoky, highland single malt.

As I thought that, a highland single malt appeared, so that didn't suck.

Helen organized a large stack of books from every conceivable topic and genre you can imagine.

Fantasy fiction.

Biographies.

Self-help.

Even *Cajun cookbooks.*

I asked if I could take that last one with me. I'd always wanted to learn how to make a *Crawfish etouffee* before descending into complete oblivion.

I also needed a pause before I went any further.

I told Ana-Maria to get to know Binati and Helen and see what was happening here, while I pulled Mel off to the side.

"Ok, I have a million questions."

"What else is new?"

"True. But I need to know a few things first. What ever happened to the Mermaid and Shanthi? When I was pulled away from you guys, you all seemed to be lighting up with sparks. What was up with that?"

"It was beyond anything I can describe. It was everything. It was all of us coming home."

"Home? Nah, fuck that. It was all of you coming into an illusion. I know what home really is."

"Why, because he told you?"

"Yes, but I also intuitively know."

"You know nothing, Jon Snow."

Brownie points for the *Game of Thrones* reference. Mel always knew just what to say.

"Sean, you're repeating his talking points. Trust me, I used to as well. You know that about me. We discussed it forever. But I'm telling you, he's wrong. Whatever he's telling you is a lie. I've been home. It's grander than anything you can begin to wrap your mind around."

"Ok, let's park this for a second. Tell me, what happened to the others?"

"They went on missions to bring others home too; to rescue them from 2020."

"There's only one way to leave 2020."

"With him, right? No, there are others."

"There aren't others. His way is the only way that brings 2020 to a permanent and uncompromising end. He's the only one who can free them all from lockdowns. He's the only one who can free them from isolation."

"You don't really believe that. If you did, you wouldn't be here."

"You stepped in and brought me here, remember?"

"Again, it was your choice to come with me. You didn't have to but you did because you knew you were meant to be here. You knew Ana-Maria was too."

"So, what is here?"

"You'll find out. You are a part of something bigger than you can imagine right now. So are all of us. It will all become clear to you, I promise. You can't understand it right now but trust me when I say this - the Mermaid is also liberating everyone from 2020. She is not doing it his way. She was able to see the path when she reunited with Shanthi. The spark lit up a path for her that was closed off. Now she's lighting paths for others."

"How? By inviting them all to jam with her in her silent disco?"

Mel laughed.

"Something like that. But that's her part to play in all this. I have mine. Ana-Maria has hers. Binati has hers as well. As does Helen…and you have yours."

"What's mine?"

"Talk to Binati."

Thanks for kicking the can down the road again.

I swear, it was like talking to lawyers with these people.

You also laughed as I was getting the run-around. Again, I would have done the same. I've always been a bit of a sadist when it came to this kind of stuff.

You told me to listen to Mel.

You told me to talk to Binati.

You were also telling me how this next part was important.

"Mel, one more thing...how did you know you'd find me in Spain?"

"I've always known you'd be there. Everything happens in the perfect time and place."

Whatever experience she had in that living room seemed to give her a certain sense of clarity.

Mel wasn't a stoic Buddha by any stretch, but she seemed considerably more knowledgeable about all this then when I left her in that living room.

Something about that scene with Shanthi and the Mermaid must have really made quite an impact.

"Come on. Let's go. Binati doesn't like to be kept waiting."

I walked back into the main room of the basement where Binati, Helen and Ana-Maria were gathered around a large table with a stack of books, but also a map.

A big map.

It kind of looked like a war room from an old World War Two movie. You know the ones, right? The giant map where the Generals are all gathered around and plotting?

Do you remember war movies?

I asked Binati what was happening, and she said, "Come on, man. Don't be coy. You know what we're doing."

...and, on some level, I did.

The thing about this place was...like I was telling you, we all somehow knew everything in the deepest corners of our subconscious. We knew each other's names and stories, but we knew even more than that somehow.

Ana-Maria knew Mel, even though she asked me who she was. She knew Binati and Helen too and they knew her.

There was an instant connection among everyone, but also everything. I felt I'd been in this library before too, but couldn't tell you how.

Even though I intuitively knew what came next, I still wanted Binati to say it, because she had a great way with words, and her accent was awesome.

I'd always been a sucker for a good Indian accent.

"It's a Gujarati accent, you dolt!", she insisted.

Wow, did I say the quiet part out loud...or could she read my thoughts?

This place was stranger than the West Village at 3 a.m.

Binati was singular. A sharp wit and intellect that usually takes many lifetimes to accumulate, but she seemed to have them all in her 20s. As I spent more time in this place, I started to understand how that was possible. I was reminded of the conversation the Shadow and I had, where he talked about our consciousness simply being a filter for all that is.

Also, Binati had a sharper filter than most. Her consciousness was able to process and interpret more of what "was" than nearly anyone I'd ever met. It was belied with a strong curiosity about everything.

Like that word, belied? Huh?

Told you I was upping my vocab game.

As I got to the table, the time dilation thing happened again.

Binati was getting ready to point to the map, then everything slowed to an almost eternal crawl.

Within this space, I got to truly know Binati.

"I guess this is our time to get acquainted, yeah?", she said.

"Looks like it. You first."

"There's not much to tell really. I was always a loner. I wanted to avoid the craziness of my family and the people around me. So I buried myself in books. This was my way of connecting with the outside world. This was how I met Helen. This was how I learned Japanese, and all about physics and geopolitics and everything else. Over time, I read them all. All the ones I could find anyway."

I saw sparks lighting up around Binati as she was talking about these books.

I needed to know more.

"What was it about Japanese specifically that drew you in?"

"I loved the culture and the imagery. I always wanted to find some Japanese guy to settle down with."

"Like a Samurai warrior?"

You just shook your head.

"You really *have* never left New York."

"Nope."

"No, man. A real Japanese guy. You know, who's familiar with electricity and such things...and one who preferably has a cat."

"So, these books are your way of finding this guy?"

"My books are a way of finding everything. 2020 is eating away at this place, don't you see? It's shutting off stories and thoughts and possibilities. Every day, volumes of books disappear. I've devoted my entire life to preserving them, any way I can."

"...and that's how you ended up as the, what, the 'Steward' of the library? Or is it 'Stewardess'? What's the proper term?"

"Oh, I could give a shit about any of that. Call me whatever you'd like."

"Got it. I admire you, Binati."

"Why? I don't like being admired. Don't make this weird, ok?"

"...because you have a thirst for knowledge. You want to learn more. You have your eyes and heart open to the world. All I ever cared about was not getting jumped on my way home from school, making sure Nana wasn't upset about something or another, and otherwise making enough money to scratch by. I never had any real curiosity about anything."

"Of course, you did. You just never pursued it. Your mind always wandered. You always wanted to know more. You just never did a damn thing about it. You sat on your lazy ass and let life pass you by."

"Direct, aren't you? I appreciate that."

"I know how to talk to people from New York. Remember, I read lots of books."

"I suppose it's true on some level. I never thought there was a bigger picture to explore, because, well, I just didn't."

"That's a cop-out, man. You were just too chickenshit to expand your horizons, like those basement-dwelling neckbeard trolls on Reddit. I don't say this to condemn you. I'm just being honest. You already know this. You always had the power to tell him to fuck off and go be someone else, do something else, and pursue what you wanted in life...and you know you did! You were just too scared. So you blamed everyone and everything for your situation, including him. *Especially* him."

Damn. Binati was dropping some serious bombs. Normally I'd have snapped at someone who talked to me like that and told them off, because they hit a nerve.

You know how it goes. The closer to the truth they get, the more defensive the response.

But somehow, I knew I needed to hear this. Coming from Binati, it was strangely ok.

Maybe it was the Indian accent.

"Gujarati."

"Stop doing that! Can you at least let me pretend you can't hear what I'm thinking?"

"Sorry. Carry on."

"Ok, well, this library...let me guess, it contains stories of everything that exists, and will exist?"

"Something like that. We create this as we go, you know? It's not a fixed thing. Our conversation right now is being written in a book, that will one day be a part of this library."

"That's pretty meta."

"Of course it is. That's also why Mel brought you here by the way. This is a continuation of your story, and I'm here to introduce you to more. You think his way is the only one. But the books will open your mind to other possibilities...to the mission you have. You and Ana-Maria both. You ready to find out?"

"As ready as I'll ever be!"

I put on a brave face.

I wasn't ready for shit.

Binati pointed on the map to France and she simply said, "*Vive la resistance*!"

"Great, Binati. So I'm going back to the 1940s to be a part of the French resistance movement against the Nazis? Can I go to Cancun instead and resist another Margarita before noon? Is that on the table?"

"Shut up and listen, ok?", Binati said.

Mel enthusiastically nodded in agreement that I needed to shut up.

At least Ana-Maria and Helen found it funny.

Not so much you.

You agreed that I needed to shut up and listen.

"This isn't about the French Resistance. It's simply a metaphor like all other things. The Nazi occupation of France was the best metaphor I could find for 2020. It was suppression of all thought, freedom, creativity, love and joy in favor of dogma, rigidity, the illusion of control, the extinguishing of flames and the destruction of the spirit. He was responsible for all of it. He thought it was the best way to inflict his vision on a large-scale."

"The Shadow?"

"No, Justin Bieber. Of course, the Shadow, you fuckshit!"

"In fairness, Bieber would have done the same."

There were crickets in the room for that one. Tough crowd.

"We have our own resistance to mount. This is the only way we leave 2020."

"What kind of resistance, Binati?", Ana-Maria asked.

You could tell this type of talk was getting her nervous.

Ana-Maria was a pacifist and hated the idea of conflict of any kind.

"We're resisting him", Binati continued, "We're resisting the destruction of everything we've created together."

"Ok, but how? I'm not going to fight anyone."

"Ana, fighting is a primitive expression of anxiety and aggression. This is a different kind of fight. We can only defeat destruction with creation. We can only defeat despair with imagination. We can only defeat isolation with connection."

"So...what do we do?"

"You and Sean each have a part to play in finding the others who can help us; those who have wrestled with him before and know how to stand up to him. The happy horseshit types are no use to us right now. We need warriors. We need people who've been in the ring with this guy and won't back down."

"Why us? Why are we the ones to find them?"

"You just are. I'm simply a conduit for this message. These aren't my rules. These are our rules. We created them together. You know that we did."

"Yes, I believe I do."

I saw Ana-Maria start to slowly illuminate during this conversation. There was something about this she had been waiting for. This was the grand mission of connection she'd always thought about. This was now it.

Something also hit me in that moment.

The Mermaid talked about "the others" when we were in her kitchen.

Maybe these were the others I was meant to find?

"Ok", I asked, "Where do we find them? What do we do when we find them?"

"Don't worry about that. You'll know when you get there", said Helen, "They're waiting for you too and they don't even know it yet. But when you arrive, they'll also know what to do."

"Do I organize them into a banner of a formal resistance? Do we gather on the fields of Bannockburn and charge the English King?"

More crickets. Not a lot of *Braveheart* fans up in this mug.

"Sean, look" said Binati, "I don't know how to tell you this, but it's very important that you go on this part of the journey with an open mind. Things aren't as they appear. You simply need to go with the flow, ok?"

"Yeah...that's not exactly my strong suit."

"No shit! That's why you need to do this. This isn't supposed to be easy. What you and Ana-Maria are about to embark on has ramifications beyond anything you can begin to wrap your mind around. This resistance flows through you, ok?"

"Through me? Why me?"

"So many questions. It just does. You're the centerpiece of this whole thing for some reason. So just listen and learn and maybe try to have a little fun on the way, ok? You can do this."

"What about Ana-Maria?"

"She already knows the part she has to play."

Ana-Maria looked pensive, but also understood. As confused as I was, Ana-Maria had clarity enough to know this was the moment she'd been waiting her whole life for.

Even if this place wasn't "life" anymore, it was still her moment.

I was significantly less settled.

"Ok, Binati. This whole thing has made me dizzy already, so what's some more ridiculousness? Where do we start?"

"Wherever you'd like. Choose.", said Binati, as she showed me all the books that Helen laid out on the other table.

"What do you mean, choose? I'm going inside of a book? This is a cheap knock-off of the *Neverending Story* plot if this is how it's going down."

"Dude, you're killing me with the referential material from the 80s. That movie though had a very true theme. What's in these books is real. It's all real. It's all a product of thought and creation, as is our entire reality. What you read in a book on this table is no less real than the conversation you and I are having now, or the grief you felt when you lost your Nana, or the air that hit your face when you jumped from that building. It's all real. We created it all. Now he's trying to get us to destroy it. We can't let that happen."

I looked at you like, hey, is she for real?

You nodded. You were definitely on Team Binati.

"Ok, man, let's go. It's time to get to work. What book is it going to be?"

"What's this one about, poetry?"

Ana-Maria looked like she'd just seen a ghost.

"I know that book", she said, "I wrote that book."

"I didn't know you were an author?"

"I'm not...but I wrote that book. I can't explain it. Turn to page 31. It's about Kelsey, isn't it?"

Sure enough. It started with, "...and there Kelsey stood, under the waterfall..."

"I know her. I wrote her. I created her. But she's also real...and she created me."

I think I had my answer.

We needed to meet Kelsey.

She was going to be our first warrior.

Chapter 7: Chasing Waterfalls

I'll level with you. I'd never been inside a book before. This was going to be a new experience. It was just like swiping right on Tinder for the first time. You hope for the best, but are expecting a catastrophe.

I looked over to Mel and inquired if she was coming with.

"No. This isn't my part to play. You and Ana-Maria need to do this yourselves."

"Mel, I can't do this without you."

"You won't have to. I'll never leave you. I promise. You will see me again, whether you like it or not. But I can't come with on this part of the journey. I have other things to tend to."

Ok then.

Helen? Binati?

Nope.

They would remain back at base camp. Someone had to tend to the library. If they left it, it would decay and eventually become a part of the Shadow's realm.

Shadow's realm.

It sounds cool and mysterious, doesn't it?

Oh, right.

I've got to defeat him and save all of creation or something.

This was the part that was really strange about all of it. You and I talked about it at great length while it was happening, remember?

On one hand, I really wanted to go with him.

I wanted *nothing*.

The allure of his offer was incredibly powerful.

On the other hand, everything about them all just felt right. They all felt like family. I felt I had to go with them too.

You encouraged me with everything you had to follow them.

The tug of war happening inside me, between you on one side, and him on the other, was really powerful.

"Now look", said Binati, "Remember that this won't be what you're expecting, so go in with an open mind, ok?"

I hated it when people told me stuff like that. It's the same shit Laura once said before she took me to that horrible vegan restaurant in Chelsea.

I asked Binati if we could take the phone booth into the book and she said, "Sean, you really need to get off this 80s kick, ok?"

Binati handed me the book and wished me luck, and Ana-Maria placed her hand on it as well.

We both gave each other the, "Well, shit, here we go!" look.

Mel nodded with a confident smile.

So did Helen.

So did you.

So did the empanada guy from Marbella.

Wait, how the fuck did he end up here?

Anyway, as we clenched the book, we felt a force starting to pull us.

The book became larger and larger, and soon engulfed the entire room. The room itself became the book, and the pages began flowing through us the way goldfish swim in an aquarium. We held each other's hands tightly to make sure we ended up in the same place, and not in some disparate corners of this story.

A vortex within the pages opened up and sucked us in, with the number 31 appearing all over the place.

I thought, "31? Are we in some kind of Reggie Miller tribute video? That guy used to kill the Knicks."

After traveling for what felt like an indeterminate period of time, we were both spit out onto the side of a lake.

A little dizzy and out of sorts, we asked each other if we were ok, and tried to get our bearings.

"Ana, what is this place?"

"It's the lake."

"I got that much. But where?"

"I don't know exactly. Just that it's the lake where the waterfall is. And it's important for us to be here."

You agreed with Ana-Maria that this was an important place for me to be. You told me to go along with what came next, and, this time, I should observe more than speak.

No easy task for a New Yorker...but you knew that too.

I glanced around to get a better sense of what this place was and what we had to do next, and after a few minutes of searching, I found it.

The waterfall.

It was one of the more incredible sights I'd ever seen. It flowed powerfully yet gently at the same time, over a rocky cliff into the lake.

The water was clear and sparkling. The sun was beaming into it and filling its essence.

There was a rainbow embedded within the waterfall which was stunning.

Underneath the waterfall, immersed in that rainbow...was Kelsey.

She had long, straight red hair, the reddest I'd ever seen on anyone, including Irish Pete's sister, who was no slouch in the redhead department herself.

But Kelsey's red hair was striking.

Almost otherworldly.

"Yo! What up peeps?" she shouted at us from under the waterfall.

Can't say I expected that.

"Is it time?" she asked.

Time for what?

I looked to Ana-Maria for answers but she didn't have any.

I looked to you and you told me to focus on Kelsey. You weren't here to spoon-feed me answers. This journey was one where I had to come to them on my own.

The only thing I knew with absolute surety was that everywhere I went, everyone I met was important.

So...I just went to the source.

"Time for what, Kelsey?"

"The exhibit. Ana-Maria, you've been planning this forever!"

What exhibit? A piece of indigenous art? A boat show? I wasn't a rich enough prick for a boat show.

Ana-Maria didn't seem to know what she was talking about either, at least at the moment.

"Don't you remember, Ana-Maria? You helped me create this. You and the other poets."

"But I'm no poet!"

"Of course, you are. Your art is poetry. When you were wrestling him, you had this idea of an expo where we could shine the light of this art everywhere. You thought if you put on an expo of art, he would leave you alone for a while."

"But nothing came of that! It was just another one of my stupid fantasies like all the rest. A pipe dream that led to nothing."

"Did it?", said Kelsey, "Look over there."

Kelsey pointed towards the rocks against the bank of the lake.

Art was suddenly appearing everywhere.

The rock wall on the lake turned into a gallery of everything imaginable.

Unicorns.

Multicolor designs of landscapes.

Conceptual paintings of people.

Ana-Maria was enthralled.

"Kelsey, did you create all this?"

"We all did."

You had a big smile as you saw this.

The biggest I'd ever seen on you.

I also looked around for the Shadow to gauge his reaction, as this surely must have chapped his ass, but he was nowhere to be found.

I asked Kelsey who this exhibit was for, and she said everyone.

"Ok", I wondered, "Then where is everyone?"

"Alone. Disconnected. Trapped in 2020."

I noticed her energy immediately shift...and the Shadow reappeared right next to her.

"I created this art for all of them, because they all created it for me. So did you. Both of you. Because they need it now more than ever. It's their only ticket out of 2020. Ana, you unlocked this in me, don't you remember?"

Ana-Maria couldn't reconcile this in her mind.

She believed she'd never done anything for anyone. The thought of having done nothing in the world tortured her, and haunted her.

"No, Kelsey. I didn't. This was all you."

"Ana, don't you see? That's what he wants you to think. That's how he gets you. That's how he gets all of us."

The Shadow was clearly getting agitated at this point. You could tell that him and Kelsey had a long history and there was something about her that really unnerved him.

"Ana, you connected this art to everyone. You saved us with this. You saved us from him."

Ana-Maria only remembered her art as something she'd scribbled here and there. It never occurred to her that she had a hand in anything this elaborate.

"What are you talking about, Kelsey?"

"You wrote this. You imagined this. Your love of art created me. It created this waterfall. It created everything you see here."

"So you're not real?"

"I'm every bit as real as you are."

Ok, was I on mushrooms?

What the hell was going on here?

I feel like I have been asking that a lot over the past few…

Days? Weeks? Months? Years?

I didn't know anymore. Legitimately.

The depth of the conversations. The intensity of the experience. The fusing of myself and the situation around me.

It was…unto itself.

But in this moment, Ana-Maria was out of sorts too.

"Tell me how I created you, Kelsey. I need to know."

"Do you remember the session we had? The art therapy session where we used the colors to represent my emotions, wants, needs, thoughts and desires?"

"We never had that. I only wrote that."

"But that's how it happened. That's how I happened. That's how this happened."

"So…you're saying by writing about you, I brought you to life."

"More. You brought *them* to life too."

"Who's *them*?"

"The other ones who were lost. The others who were in his grip. The others who were on their own ledges. The ones whose flames had gone out and whose sparks were extinguished. You were dreaming one night about human connection, and you conjured me up. You thought about an alter ego who expressed herself as an artist…and I was born that night."

"But you're real. You're looking at me right now."

"Ana, I conjured you too."

"What do you mean?"

"I've never experienced this world before. I'm from another time and another place. A place that you can't understand right now. But believe me when I tell you; you're a part of everything here. You were the spark that lit me up. You were the spark that created this art."

"It's beautiful, Kelsey…but I don't understand the point. It's just art on a wall. What can that possibly do against him?"

"Everything. He has no power in the face of art. Even the darkest of art. Art simply deflects him. It removes his mystique. It calls him out. It acknowledges him."

"That's why the art has demonic imagery?"

"Of course. He's no demon. We only think he is because that is the perception he helps us build. Art shatters that perspective. I battled him forever. You know that. You created me to battle him, don't you remember?"

Ana-Maria needed to sit down as she felt faint.

In one rushing moment of clarity, she understood it all.

She had already fulfilled her mission without ever realizing it.

Her online art therapy classes for people around the world unleashed their sparks. It connected them to others through those sparks. It created characters and worlds and life.

It channeled the energy of all that exists into manifesting even more.

It blinded out the darkness.

It kept the Shadow at bay for countless people.

That's why he wanted her so badly. She was one of the spark lighters.

It also seemed like she needed to meet me to bring her here.

Somehow, I was connected to all this and needed to be the conduit to bring her to Binati and Helen, which would eventually bring her here.

She didn't need to recruit the warriors in the fight after all.

She'd already created so many of them.

...and now, Kelsey was telling her to find the rest.

To understand her work.

To continue to light their sparks.

To light them so brightly that the Shadow could never extinguish them again.

Ana-Maria's creations were the artists of the world. She created Kelsey, and Kelsey in turn created her. They created each other to fight him. They did all this to keep creation alive.

...and he hated them for it.

He couldn't subdue Kelsey so he tried with Ana-Maria, because if he got her, he'd get them both and all the rest eventually.

The absence of one would be felt by everyone.

And then all the artists, already prone to his charms, would be easy prey.

One by one, they'd build their roads to him and become his. Kurt Cobain did. So did Robin Williams and Greg Giraldo and so many others.

Their luminous sparks would be erased forever.

"What do we do now, Kelsey?" Ana-Maria wondered aloud.

"We find the others. The other artists. The poets. The magicians. We bring them here. To the expo. We join our sparks together and shine so brightly that he can never hurt any of us again. Together, he can't touch us. Together, we'll leave 2020."

"How do we find them?"

"The Mermaid is already helping us. She's connecting us all."

"She is? I've only heard of this Mermaid from Sean and Mel."

"Yeah, she's doing her thing. You'll see. Trust me. In the meantime, we have our own ways of reaching people."

"How?"

"Look over there."

Kelsey pointed to one of the paintings on the rocks.

It was a spiral that seemed to go on for eternity.

"You see that? It's the sacred spiral. It's a symbol of the resistance. It's a symbol that we're here. It symbolizes that we're going to keep going."

"I see, Kelsey. Tell me, what if enough people don't see it? How do we reach everyone?"

"They're already looking. There's a world full of people out there who are trapped. They can't shake free of 2020. They're all in his grip. But they're looking for us. I promise you; we'll find them."

As Kelsey was speaking, Ana-Maria felt the power of her words. And the message behind them. She needed to go with Kelsey. She needed to find the other creatives and help them leave 2020 so they wouldn't end up like Cobain and the rest.

She wanted to make sure they wouldn't end their lives at his hands. She wanted to make sure they could bring their sparks to the world.

...whichever world that may be.

Kelsey and Ana-Maria joined in a scene reminiscent of the one in Shanthi's living room.

These were two tortured, pained souls, half in the light and half in the darkness, who joined in a way that formed nothing but light.

They both had sparks radiating from them. Light poured from their pores and spread all around them.

Together, they formed an impenetrable wall of pure energy that the Shadow was unable to come near.

It was beautiful, and inspiring.

And yet...

...I felt the same hollow feeling as I did before.

You told me to let myself be inspired by Kelsey and Ana-Maria and to see the beauty of what they were creating here, and I did.

I really did.

I saw what you were trying to do, and why Binati and Helen sent me here.

They wanted me to connect with the kind of creativity I'd been ignoring my whole life, because he stomped out my spirit every step of the way.

They needed me to reunite Ana-Maria and Kelsey, and have them go off on their own mission to create magic into the unknown.

I saw it. I truly did. It was beautiful and inspiring. But...still...I felt him tugging on my sleeve.

I couldn't shake the feeling that he was still somehow going to win.

"Of course I'm going to win", he said, appearing next to me.

"What did you think? Did you really think Ana-Maria was the only one who matters? Did you think I can't overcome the temporary loss of Kelsey? I promise you, they'll both be back. They can't form that wall of light forever. When they're alone again, they're mine."

"You seemed pretty intent on getting Ana-Maria. This is a bigger loss for you than you're letting on, tough guy."

"It's a temporary setback. I have all of eternity to win this. Do you?"

He was a real insolent son of a bitch like that.

That said, I knew he had a point. I'd felt it many times in my own life.

When there's stillness and silence, there's only him. There's only the darkness. That's when he strikes.

This is true for all of us...especially people like Kelsey and Ana-Maria.

They'd each wrestled with him repeatedly over the course of their lives. He had them both on the brink of suicide more times than either could count.

Yet, every time he had them on that edge, they'd create a work of art.

Then, just like a military flashlight, it would blind him.

He'd retreat immediately from the light. The light from their art would also reach others, like the starlight of distant suns reaching across the galaxy.

Just like that, each time the others would feel that light, it would ignite their sparks. It would inspire them to create their own art, which brought each of them back from the ledge as well.

It created a ripple effect.

The most beautiful ripple effect in the realest sense of the word.

Now, working together, they could create a large enough ripple effect that could thwart his plans and dismantle 2020.

They could restore the way we used to see each other - as other human beings much like ourselves. They would see that we were just beings to connect with, to sing with, paint with, make music with. That we were not conduits of doom. That we were not dangerous, crude biological weapons to be feared.

It hit me in that moment: **We could all leave 2020 together.**

This thought, just this thought alone, made me feel stronger. Nothing was a greater threat to the Shadow or his end game.

I saw his conundrum.

The very existence of creativity was an affirmation of life and living and all that we were. It was the exit ramp for this collective nightmare.

"You get it now", he said, "But ask yourself this. Let's say they find the others. Let's say they light all those sparks. Let's even say they reach everyone. How many of them are there, really? You think everyone can compose a poem? Or a painting? Or a song? Or a joke? The rest...all of them...still see my truth. They always have. The artists are simply their distractions to pretend I don't exist. But there's no pretending anymore. 2020 has lifted the veil of illusion once and for all."

I knew he was right on some level.

Still, I had to find the others. If it were just the artists leaving 2020, what did that mean for the rest of us left behind? Why should a painter be liberated from this nightmare but an accountant remain in his bear grip?

If you couldn't create a painting, were you destined for a hollow existence that led to suicide?

2020 had turned everyone into tortured, depressed, suicidal artists...minus the art.

So what other weapons did they have in their arsenal to fight him, if not creativity?

It didn't add up.

If we truly co-created all this together as he suggested, and as I was slowly beginning to understand... why do only a few get to leave? We wouldn't do that to each other, would we? Create a segregation system among us of creatives and non-creatives?

I had to find out.

I owed it to Ana-Maria and Kelsey.

I owed it to Mel and the Mermaid and Shanthi.

I owed it to Binati and Helen who had enough faith in me to send me on this journey.

Shit, I even owed it to Cortez and Irish Pete.

And Sam.

And Laura.

And that asshole with the goatee.

...but I had no idea what to do from here. I thought this was the first stop on some mapped-out trip. I guess Mel and Binati were right when they said this wouldn't go as I expected.

However, I suddenly remembered the words "mapped out trip" and I immediately felt myself getting pulled again into another vortex.

I looked over, and this one was created by you.

You told me to follow it, that I saw what I needed to see here, but that the next place would open my eyes even more.

You ushered me into the vortex and followed right alongside me. We were sucked in there together.

This one was really, really strong. The ride this time was bumpy like a hot air balloon cruising through a tornado...or the F train to Queens.

This vortex spit me out into a dusty, windy siding on a desert road. From what I could tell, and what I'd seen in pictures, it looked like the Southwest.

Nevada, maybe?

More likely Arizona.

It was a scorching hot, windy day with the powerful sun beating down on me, as the asphalt burned the soles of my shoes. It must have been at least 105°F degrees out there.

In the distance, I saw a red Corvette speeding down the road. It had the top down and it was absolutely flying. Lucky for them, there were no state troopers in sight.

But when the car reached me, it came to a dead and immediate stop.

Damn. Nice brakes. I want the name of their mechanic.

In the car were a couple who looked to be in their mid-50s. They both rocked silver hair and each exuded a glow of...for lack of a better term, "easiness."

I could only define this easiness as the ease of living and peace.

They looked like human manifestations of Key West. They were settled in life, happy as hell and not a care in the world.

They were a couple of fellow Americans named Greg and Judy.

"Hop in dude, we've been waiting for you" said Judy.

I looked over at Greg for clarity.

"Don't look at me, man. She's the boss. Hop in. We're about to hit the winery, then have a lot of sex."

Well then.

Chapter 8: Feeling the Love

The feeling of a Corvette speeding through the desert is unto itself. The hot, dry air blowing in your face. The feeling of freedom. The anticipation of the destination ahead.

"Guys, where are we going?"

"The Singh winery."

"Where's that?"

"The Shenandoah foothills in Virginia."

"Wait, we're driving from Arizona to Virginia?"

"Yeah," said Greg, "Don't worry though, we've got a good tailwind and are riding the Jet stream. We'll be there in a couple hours, max."

I wish I had a meme of that woman with the "Wat" caption...but hey, par for the course around here.

"So, what brings you two here?"

"Same as you, man. We're leaving 2020."

"How can you leave a year in a corvette?"

They both got a good chuckle.

"You know how."

More riddles and assumptions; just shoot me now.

"Greg, how is going to a winery the same as leaving 2020?"

"How is it not?"

"You can't answer a question with a question, brother."

"Sure I can. I survived the Wicked Witch of Southern Missouri. I can do whatever I damn well please!"

Judy smiled and nodded.

"Wait...you survived who?"

"The Wicked Witch of Southern Missouri. You heard of her, right? She's the redhead they talk about in tales to scare all the children in the realm."

The only redheads I ever knew were Kelsey and Irish Pete's sister...and neither were a witch. That said, Irish Pete's sister definitely had her moments after a few too many shots of Jameson, but she was no witch.

"Yeah, man. All the kids hear about her. We tell them about her to scare them into behaving. The best part is I was actually married to her!"

"Ah. So, you meant not a real, actual witch but a metaphorical one. Let me guess, she had a good lawyer who cleaned out your 401k and took the ottoman for good measure?"

"She's a Witch, man. A real one. Witches don't need lawyers. She had much more powerful things at her disposal than that. She had deception and tunnels."

Again, with these tunnels. I felt like I was going to have to start paying tolls if someone mentioned that word again.

"She helped us build one throughout our marriage together. I didn't notice it at the time. It just slowly built up. One thing after another; everything that I loved, she talked me out of doing. Traveling, flying, going to football games; all of it. It started out gradually, and over time, it just became normal. She chipped away at me, one piece at a time."

"Why did you stay with her then?"

"When you're in the middle of it, you can't see anything outside of it. I had blocked off all communication. I couldn't speak to her from my heart because she trapped all my energy. She stifled me at every turn. It reduced my spirit to rubble."

"How did you escape?"

"Judy freed me."

Judy flashed a big smile and said, "Bet your sweet ass I did!"

I, of course, had to know how.

"Well, before I met Greg, I was with an evil wizard of my own."

"Let me guess, from Southern Missouri?"

I laughed.

I was decidedly the only one who laughed.

You shook your head again and told me to listen to Judy.

"No. This one was from the Yinzer realm."

"Pittsburgh?"

"Where?"

"Never mind. Carry on. Evil wizard. Yinzer realm."

"He trapped me too. He entrapped me in a place where my thoughts, hopes, dreams and passions were confined. He tried to convince me I could never escape either."

"Why would he do that? To what end?"

"Couldn't tell you. The guy was just a real dick. A narcissistic dirtbag. I wish I had something more profound to say than that."

"Nah. It's good enough for me. Tell me, how did you guys break out of your funk? This is the part that's really interesting to me. I was stuck in one of my own places for as long as I could remember and could never get out."

"We broke each other out. Even though we were both trapped, suffocated and slowly dying, we felt something outside trying to break through. Something outside was trying to get in. It wasn't easy, that's for damn sure. The Witch and the Wizard did everything they could to keep us in. They both said how we were nuts for trying to escape. They threatened us with all kinds of things if we dared look for ways out."

This witch and wizard sounded an awful lot like *him*.

Were they his agents?

I tried looking for him, to ask if he had a hand in this, but he wasn't in the car with us.

"So, what ended up happening?"

"I somehow felt Greg's energy reach me, and he found mine reach him. To this day we couldn't tell you exactly how it happened. But somehow, we always knew about each other. We always felt drawn to each other. We somehow always knew each of us would be the other's way out."

"How?"

"I saw a vague shape of Greg appear one day. It was faint and hard to connect with. But I felt a deep, strong connection to his energy. He felt the same for mine. He told me that the witch had him sentenced to an early death, but not the kind you think of. It was a soul death, where she was about to extinguish the last remaining spark he had. Only I could help him. So that night I started diggin' out. I tried leaving. Oh, that bastard Wizard tried to stop me. He did everything he could to stop me."

"But he wasn't successful?"

"He almost was. There were so many days when he made me think there was no way out. He made me believe my life was going to be chained to his. He really made me think that he would own my energy forever. But something kept me going. That something was Greg. I just knew he was out there waiting for me."

"Wow. That's the stuff they make movies about."

"Yep. Or write books about."

A weird sensation came over me when she said that last part.

Anyway, I needed to see how Greg and Judy fit into this puzzle.

They were both able to escape his grip somehow; the grip he exercised on them through his proxies.

It became apparent that he worked through proxies all over the world. Narcissists and those like them...all the people who create the conditions that make you feel hopeless and turn to him.

All these malicious people in the employ of the Shadow make you feel utterly broken. They don't create, they destroy. They don't inspire, they cage. They don't heal, they annihilate.

Talking to Greg and Judy also reminded me of the conversation I had with Mel about the conventions, and it was reinforced by the conversation I had with the Shadow.

A jailbreak was possible through others who didn't destroy, but rather created. Others who built you up. Others who stood with you. Others who brought out the best in you.

It was definitely possible.

Connection with others, at least with the right ones, helped shatter the walls and let the light in.

It was still entirely theoretical to me. But seeing more and more people talk about this was starting to get my attention.

Still, I needed some philosophical questions answered because, like clockwork, just as I was starting to get some revelations about this, he showed up and started whispering in my ear.

I turned to Judy and asked, "Judy. Why did you really want to escape? Didn't it occur to you and Greg; didn't it occur to you too that escaping from the Witch and the Wizard would lead you to each other...just to build new confines of your own? Weren't you both getting into the same bullshit? Wasn't it all just a different face to wake up to in the morning?"

They looked at each other for a second, then Greg said, "Judy, you want to take this one?"

She looked back and said, "Nah, man. This baby's all yours."

Greg peered up at the rearview mirror as if to look at me directly.

"So, it's like this. Of course, we've got plenty of our own shit to deal with. We have lots of fights and bad days. That's life, man. That's how this all goes. But it's different this time around because the other perspectives with the Witch and Wizard were static, you see? The Wicked Witch built my perspective to only have one exit; one way out which was my soul death. There were no other paths I could take. With Judy though, the perspective has no singular destination. If I want to take it to a different place, her energy helps shift its trajectory with me. The very same for her. It's fluid. It keeps expanding every day."

"All that expansion...and you didn't even need a city permit?"

Crickets. I'm glad I didn't quit my day job.

"Every time Judy and I have a new idea, we follow it. This new perspective expands to let more light in. Every time we travel to a new destination, it expands. Every time we get a honeymoon suite and use prosecco to..."

"Ok, TMI, dude."

"You get the point. Unlike with the others, we're not on a fixed path. Together, we expand our horizons. We explore new possibilities. We light each other's sparks and free our energy to go where it needs to go. We encourage that energy to fly. We encourage the energy to grow; to flourish."

I think I was starting to get the essence of what they were saying.

It was clear that the Witch and the Wizard were simply acting as agents of the Shadow.

He deputized them to do his dirty work.

He used these people to crush the spirits of others.

He enabled them to build perspectives of hopelessness and resignation to a slow, meandering, meaningless death, where no light of joy, inspiration or creativity was allowed to enter.

...the same way he's deputized the Doomers of 2020. The ones who've taken to social media every day to tell us all how hopeless it was. To plant hourly seeds of catastrophe. To convince us there was no tomorrow.

...the same way he nearly deputized me to do the same with Ana-Maria.

It occurred to me that this was happening all over the world. I just never realized it until now.

It's not just him.

There's no way he could do it all on his own.

He has an army, a literal fucking army, of people who are in his employ. People who do his bidding. Individuals who crush spirits and extinguish sparks and cage energy.

I blamed politicians for doing it with the lockdowns. Now I know they were just a few among millions.

But...Greg and Judy broke free.

Somehow, they wrestled with his deputies and won.

"So, are you guys now free of the Witch and the Wizard forever?"

I was waiting for an answer that would bring this whole saga to a happy ending.

A perfect conclusion.

A roadmap to victory.

"Oh hell no", said Greg, "If only."

Well, so much for that.

"She'll never stop trying to cage me again. It's her mission in life. My energy threatens her existence. Every trip Judy and I take, every kiss we exchange, every good bottle of wine we enjoy, it erodes another bedrock of her existence. She hasn't gone quietly into the night, and she never will."

"So how do you deal with her?"

"I keep living, dude. I don't let it bring me down nor do I let it stop me. I accept that her presence is just a part of the whole gig."

"Don't you ever get tired of fighting, though? If you know she's never going to leave you alone, why not just acquiesce and earn yourself a little peace and quiet?"

"Sean, the *Nothing* will earn you neither peace nor quiet. A soul death isn't peaceful, despite what you may have heard. It's a torturous descent into a place of regret, disintegration and eventual nothingness. To make matters worse, it doesn't happen quickly. There's no easy way out of this. You're in for a fight either way. I choose to fight for me and I chose to fight for Judy."

"Sounds like we're all drafted into a war."

"This is the price we all agreed to pay when this all started. It's the price of admission."

"For what?"

"For everything."

I saw the sincerity in his eyes, and I saw it in Judy's. These two were light spirits, but they were dead serious about this. It was no laughing matter. They were both in the fight of their lives against the Shadow and his minions...and neither were willing to give an inch.

"Guys. I need to connect you to the others. You're going to help be the leaders of the resistance Binati was talking about."

"Oh, right, Binati sent you. How's she doing in that library of hers anyway?" asked Judy.

"As far as I can tell, she's got her shit together."

"Yeah, because Helen keeps her in check. Sometimes she needs a good talkin' to in Japanese, right?"

"You've been there? To the library in India?"

"Dude, we've been everywhere."

"You'll help me then? You'll help everyone else leave 2020? If they all saw things like you, maybe together we'll have what it takes to do this."

"Sorry, buddy. Can't help ya!"

"What the hell? What do you mean you can't help me? I was specifically sent here to draft you to..."

"Draft? What is this, Vietnam? We're headed to the winery to sit outside on a nice day and then devour each other afterwards. That's always been the plan. We picked you up to bring you to the winery. What happens after that, well, you're on your own, man."

I was pissed. This wasn't the answer I was looking for.

But you told me to settle down.

You reassured me that this was all unfolding as it needed to.

We continued on the road for another few hours, with the world speeding by at a clip I'd never seen before.

They were playing a great road trip playlist, complete with Jackson Browne and all the other great 1970s coming-of-age hits.

I felt like I need to be sporting mutton chops and a really shitty brown leather jacket to fully immerse in it.

As I had these thoughts, I actually felt the mutton chops growing in then yelled, "NO! I wasn't being literal."

"Careful", said Greg, "Those things are a bitch to shave off. You should've seen me in high school! I am surprised anyone got laid in those days looking like that!"

Judy was cracking up. So were you.

We finally arrived at the winery, and it was set in a picturesque valley with the Blue Ridge mountains in the background. The leaves were in the midst of peak foliage, as is the case with most days of Autumn.

While I still didn't quite know what this plane of existence was, if it were Heaven and I was bound to be here forever, I could certainly do a lot worse.

We entered the main tasting room, and Greg and Judy gave a big hug to the proprietor, Sue.

"Welcome back, my dear friends!", she said, "It hasn't been the same without you. Sean, I'm glad you're here too."

She knew my name. Of course she did.

"Sean, you have no idea what these two humans mean to me."

"How so?"

"First have a glass of the Mélange Blanc. This is a rather long story."

I was cool with that.

Again, I'm a sucker for Indian accents.

"Sean, you see, Judy and Greg found me at my lowest point. I was in his firm grip. I call him the *snake*. You know who I'm talking about?"

"Yes. I know exactly who you're talking about."

"It was the deepest grip I'd ever known. I'm from a place called Hyderabad, India, and my whole life was geared towards winning the affection of a man I loved more than anything in the world.

I love the idea of love. I always had. Then this man stole my heart when I was very young. However, life and circumstance took us in different directions. I tried to follow him to the ends of the Earth, but it was not to be. I simply slipped into the embrace of sadness and despair.

After many years and many travels, I returned to the city of my youth, and as I was walking to purchase some vegetables, in the distance, I saw what could only be him. The years had certainly left their imprint on his life. I saw the bags under his eyes, the grey in his hair, and he wasn't walking with the same confident posture I'd remembered from his younger years.

...but it was him. It was absolutely him. I just knew the stars had brought us back together. I knew how despite all the years of pain, all the years of heartache and all the years in the firm grip of the *snake*, my long-awaited love was at hand.

He drew closer to me, and I walked out of my way to ensure the 'chance' encounter. I bumped into his shoulder and said 'excuse me'. He stopped, looked me right in the eye, and that split-second felt like an eternity. It all simply came back to me. The butterflies, the dreams of our lives together, the intensity of my love for him. That moment was the most profound moment of my life.

He looked back into my eyes, and I eagerly awaited the words out of his mouth.

He said, 'no worries, have a nice day', and continued walking.

He didn't recognize me. I was nothing to him. I was no one. I was invisible. My heart was left on that city street, frayed and scattered around in tatters.

I returned home in tears, where the *snake* was waiting for me. He told me that this was the cost of living, and it was too high to bear. He offered me a way out of the pain. I was ready to finally take him up on his offer.

...that's when Judy and Greg arrived.

You see, I was known as the wine connoisseur of Hyderabad, and on their travels, they looked me up. I'd forgotten, in my pain, that we had a meeting scheduled for that day.

But there they were. These two happy Americans who couldn't wait to meet me were there.

Me?

Why?

They were so excited though.

They asked all about me. They inquired where I was from, what I enjoyed doing, and only after all that did we start talking about wine.

Their interest lit a spark in me that died just one hour before. After spending a few days showing them around the place, they offered me a business opportunity. I was to open a winery in the United States of America. They wanted me to create a place where we could fuse my native traditions with their soil, and create a safe haven for all those who still believed in the power of love."

"A haven for love at a winery? I don't understand."

"You see, the Singh winery isn't just any winery. It's based on the philosophy of my ancestor, Harmeet Singh. This philosophy recognizes the chaos of all creation. It also however mentions how love emerges from absolute chaos. Love is always more powerful than the chaos. It is more powerful than destruction. It's the single most creation-affirming thing that exists."

I looked over to the wall, and saw a portrait of her ancestor.

Harmeet was a formidable man. It looked like this was drawn sometime in the mid-late 19th century if I had to guess. He had a red turban and a well-kept beard, with a large smile that could fill the room. Harmeet's presence could be felt in every corner of the winery.

"You see", said Sue, "Harmeet always believed in the balance of things. We mustn't run from the chaos. That we mustn't hide from it. The *snake* will always be there to sow the seeds of chaos, and then fill us with his own brand of certainty to feel safe during the aftermath. Each of us has the power to fight the chaos that ensues. We can all use the swirling energy of creation to our advantage. We should channel the energy to love and be loved instead of following him to destruction."

This sounded a bit new age for my taste. I was waiting for her to sell me on a seminar to discover my divine and cosmic love.

I was also waiting on the tarot card reader and essential oils table.

But as Greg and Judy and I walked around the grounds and sat down at a table to enjoy the excellent wine, Sue's words made sense.

These words didn't make sense on an intellectual level. It's difficult to buy into this stuff.

...but on a deeper, visceral level. I "got" it.

There were people all around me living this out loud, in real life, in real time; especially at one crowded table right next to us.

I didn't know if this were heaven, hell, or somewhere in between, but I have to tell you, the sight of all those people together with no need for masks or social distancing was heaven enough for me.

Two of those people were Siala and Violeta.

Siala was a Kiwi from New Zealand, with a glowing South Pacific presence that let you know she was in the room. It's the best way I can describe it, but it doesn't do her justice. Siala had a way of lighting up everyone around her.

The energy she was giving off was off the charts.

Violeta had glasses, dark hair and a subtle Romanian accent. You could tell she wanted to say more, and had a lot to share, but spoke only in the moments when she felt she would truly be heard.

Siala was talking to Violeta about her husband, and how much he was grating on her nerves that day.

"But you're still with him, right?"

"Of course. Always. No matter what."

I looked over at you and asked why I'm sitting in on the kind of conversation you'd normally overhear at the nail salon.

You told me to pipe down and just listen.

"Look", said Siala, "We've been through plenty of hell and back together; like most couples, I would imagine. I love the guy through and through, no matter what. There's something about him that gives me purpose. This something lets me know what I'm going through is worth it, so I can be there for him."

"How did you know he was the one?"

"I didn't know. There wasn't any one moment. It was just a gradual thing, right? One day after the next. We overcame one thing. Then we moved on to the next. Sickness, loss, disappointment, family drama, you know; all of it. He's still the one though. I know I have something to live for every day I see him."

"I feel the same way about my dog, Puppa."

"At least you don't have to share the blanket with Puppa!"

"I don't. She gets whatever she wants. Whatever's left, she gives to me."

I found it funny that the dog called the shots. I never had a dog. Nana was allergic and there was always a good chance some idiot in the building would have fed it a chocolate just to be a spiteful ass. Those were the kinds of neighbors we had on Avenue B.

"Puppa has gotten me through so much. This year took everything from me. My job. My mental health. Whatever was left of my sanity. I wanted to give up so many times. The *dragon* would encourage me to give up and told me that my time here was over."

"The *dragon*?"

"I don't know what you call him in New Zealand."

"Oh. Right. *Him*. I don't give him a name. I refuse to give him the honor of a name."

"Well, to me, and others from Romania where I was born, he's the *dragon*. He tried taking me to *that place*...but Puppa rescued me. She wouldn't let me go. When I came home and Puppa was waiting, I knew I had a reason to keep going."

"Looks like we were both able to fight him off through our love for two slobbering creatures who eat a lot!"

Judy chimed in from the other table, "You know it!"

Greg just kept drinking.

It was the right move.

Between Greg and Judy, and Siala and Violeta, I did find something interesting.

They all mentioned fighting him without a hint of creative art in their toolbox. They weren't putting out new works of literature that would be in Binati and Helen's library, nor expressions that would be on display at Kelsey and Ana-Maria's expo.

They just had love.

Love for each other.

Love for their pets.

That was it.

Just love.

For them, that seemed to be enough.

As Siala was talking about her husband, and Violeta was petting little Puppa, both were lighting up with sparks.

"Sean", asked Siala, "Who do you love?"

This question floored me.

I really wanted to give a smart-ass answer about some band or athlete or a favorite bottle of whiskey, but I couldn't conjure up that kind of response for some reason.

So...I just answered honestly.

"No one. I love no one."

"Really?", asked Violeta, "No one? Not even a dog?"

"No. I love no one. I've never loved anyone like that. The only person I ever loved was Nana...but she's gone."

"Was there ever anyone? If you could take it all back, who would you love?", Violeta wondered.

I really had to stop at this point.

This was getting into some deeply personal shit for me.

I'd always been a loner in this department. Sure, I'd go home with the random stranger from McCabe's here and there, but I could never bring myself to love anyone...like, really love anyone because all I thought about were my parents.

They loved me, presumably. I loved them as much as a baby can love anyone. Then some drunk scumbag stole them from me.

If I ever loved anyone, something would rip them away too.

Maybe another drunk on the road.

Maybe this goddamn virus.

Maybe just old age.

One way or the other, it would happen again.

It happened with Nana.

I didn't need to endure this again.

It wasn't worth it.

I wasn't built for love.

I wasn't built for what loving someone would entail.

I just couldn't handle the pain.

I was always more afraid of living than dying, and nothing would have represented living more than taking that kind of a plunge.

Sam was the closest I ever got. She wanted it. I know she did. She talked about the future a lot. She wanted to settle down, have kids, have a mortgage, join the P.T.A., get a minivan, take the kids to soccer, all that shit.

She wanted it more than anything, and for some strange reason, she wanted it with me.

Me?

Who the hell was I to be a soccer dad?

Who the hell was I to be a good husband?

I was a borderline alcoholic with a bad temper and depression. You'd have better luck finding father-of-the-year material among the lunatics who hung out at the bus station.

Still, something about seeing Siala talk about her husband in particular, and the bond that Greg and Judy had got my mind wandering.

What if...what if I didn't chicken out with Sam?

What if I actually stayed?

What if I asked her to marry me?

What would 2020 have looked like if we endured it together?

What if she were at my side when I lost Nana?

What if I gave Nana great-grandkids?

How much would that have lit her up before she went?

I thought about it all - all the possibilities...and it started driving me crazy.

"Stop it", said Violeta, "I know what you're doing. I do it to myself too. You just need to stop it."

"Stop what?"

"Stop beating yourself up. I know you do it all the time. I used to do the same. You're not perfect. Neither am I. All we are, all we have, is our choices. You need to make peace with yours. Sam isn't coming back. You know that. So why do this? Why beat yourself up like this?"

"Because I like torturing myself. It's my favorite sport. Besides, why did you ask me about this if you already knew the answer? We can read each other's thoughts here, right? You knew about Sam. Violeta, tell me, why? Why did you bring her up?"

"I didn't. You know it wasn't her I was talking about."

"The hell it wasn't. Who else could it be? Laura? Please."

"No. Not Laura. You know who."

"Ok, I give up. Who?"

"The one who walked away."

Walked away? Who walked away? I didn't know who the....

...oh.

Right.

Of course.

Tess.

She was talking about Tess.

Tess from last December, right before all this shit went down.

I picked up a Saturday night at McCabe's because Laura and I had yet another fight and I needed something to keep my mind busy. I figured, I was going to be at McCabe's drinking one way or the other, so might as well get paid for it.

Around 9:30PM, I saw a petite brunette sitting at the end of the bar. She was there all alone, checking her phone constantly. I mean, that wasn't entirely unusual for December, 2019, but she looked antsy.

I chatted with her as she ordered a second glass of Pinot Noir, and she let me know that she'd been stood up.

That definitely sucked.

I bought her a couple glasses on the house that night. I felt bad. It's awful to get all dolled up then be left holding the bag, stuck talking to a miserable windbag like me for the evening.

She probably dodged a bullet anyway, since if this guy's idea of impressing a lady was taking her to McCabe's, he had really shitty judgement.

She told me her name was Tess, and that she was originally from California and moved to New York because she loved the vibe.

Was she a masochist?

That said, there was something about Tess that was...different. Whatever it was, it was unlike anything I ever knew.

Tess really loved the city and it radiated from her as she spoke about it. She loved the possibilities it offered. She loved the people. She loved the energy. She loved the vibrancy.

She said that every morning, she woke up and took an early stroll along the East entrance of Central Park, right at the base on 59th Street. She said she loved the way the sun rose and shone through the trees. Something about it made everything just seem perfect in her eyes.

No one talked like that at McCabe's. Ever.

Tess was a true "high on life" type. We were chatting about movies and she said her favorite was *Braveheart,* just like mine. She especially loved it because of the line, "Every man dies. Not every man really lives."

To quote the younger millennials, I felt personally attacked by that remark.

But there was something about her which really spoke to me.

Maybe she was the other side of me I always hoped to find, but never could?

Maybe she was the embodiment of what I strived to be?

Or, was she someone who didn't seem to be under his spell?

Was that it? She didn't mention him at all, which was a rare thing for anyone who ever pulled up a seat at McCabe's...or anyone in my life for that matter.

As the night went on, I could tell she was flirting with me. I wasn't the brightest bulb, but I knew that much.

Was it the loneliness of being stood up?

Was she really interested in me?

Was…well, *Mr. Wonderful* showed up right on cue. He whispered in my ear that a sweet, attractive girl like this could never be interested in a loser like me. She was flirting because she was stood up and wanted some male attention for the night and, of course, some free drinks.

How could she be interested in a moody boozebag like me?

So… I let her walk.

She got up, grabbed her coat, got to the door, then paused.

She gave me one more chance to make a move. She waited. She locked eyes with me.

That's when he whispered again, "Let her walk. You know damn well she's out of your league."

So, I listened and she walked.

I regretted it every day since.

"So," said Violeta, "If you could take it back, would you choose her?"

"Take it back? I can't take anything back. That already happened. It's done. That was in December 2019 before the whole world went to hell. There's no going back."

"No, there isn't", she said, "but there is going forward."

You told me to internalize that deeply.

You told me how if I remembered nothing else from this place, I need to remember that last line.

You were very intent that I accept that message.

Why, though?

That night of 2019 came and went. What was to be gained by thinking about it again? Is the future the past somehow? Is this a time travel saga? Is Doc Brown going to show up in his Delorean?

Being at this winery made me remember all the shots I didn't take in life.

Things could have ended up differently if I took those shots. I could have ended up here in this place with them full of love.

They left 2020 with love... and maybe, I could have too.

"Don't beat yourself up", said Aman, Sue's nephew who also worked at the winery. He had stopped by our table to pick up our glasses, "You didn't know then what you know now. It's not your fault."

Who the hell was this kid to give me life lessons?

"Everything is about connection. That's what Harmeet tried to tell us in his writings about chaos.

You see connection today as only the connection of romantic love. You torture yourself for never allowing that type of connection to come into your life. But there are other connections out there. There are so many other connections out there. These connections make up the tapestry of creation."

"Let me guess. I'm about to go to a place where I get to see this in action, right?"

"Of course, man. You're smarter than you look."

Nice.

Kid should have been an insult comic.

"I know you feel like shit right now", said Greg, "But like Aman said, there's more than one type of human connection. The love that you see here is just one brick in the castle that stands against him."

"What do you mean?"

"You see that over there?"

He pointed to a big 18-wheeler off in the distance.

"That's your ride."

You told me that you arranged the truck because there was more to see.

Siala and Violeta stood up and gave me big, warm hugs. I petted Puppa on the way out too.

Judy hugged me too and said, "You're going to be ok. Trust me on this one, you got it?"

Who was I to argue?

Then Greg slapped me on the back and said, "This is just one more stop on the ride, man. I think you'll like where you're going next. I've been there. You'll dig it."

I bid Greg and Judy an adieu, and wished them a good Prosecco-filled romp.

They smiled and nodded.

It was definitely in the cards.

I walked up to the truck on the gravel road adjacent to the winery entrance.

Driving the truck was an Aussie named Darren with thick, wavy black hair, big shades, and a plaid black and blue shirt.

"Let's go mate. I have got to get this shipment there on time."

"What's the shipment?"

"You."

Chapter 9: Punts, Pints and Pitches

Have you ever ridden shotgun in an 18-wheeler? I doubt you would have. We never discussed this but it's pretty cool. You feel the power of the rig and the road, and the other cars feel so small in comparison.

You feel invincible.

Apparently, my thoughts could also be read by Darren.

"That's what I thought too, mate. Then I jack-knifed in Queensland twelve years ago while bringing a shipment of wine from this place."

"You drove wine from Virginia to Australia?"

"Of course. Why, you don't?"

"Can't say I have. Where I'm from, they didn't build a bridge that spanned the entire Pacific Ocean."

"Sounds like that place sucks."

"It does. You're right about that. Anyway, where are we going?"

"You know where."

Uh huh.

I see another game of 20 questions was in order.

"Do I get a hint?"

"Come on, don't play dumb. You know where we're going."

I looked at you for a bit of clarification here. You dialed up this ride.

Were we going to find a true love for me to bring back to the winery? Was that how the resistance was going to be built?

I mean, sure, I could pick up some roses and learn to cook something decent.

You told me to just talk to Darren and stop asking so many questions.

"Well, alright, buddy. I'll let myself be surprised as always. So Darren, what's your story? It seems like everyone here's got one."

"How long you got?"

"You tell me, buddy. You're driving."

"We're too close for the whole story. I'd have to chuck a U-ey and start over again for the whole deal. But I'll tell you the important part. I've survived many cancers. Thirty-eight, to be precise."

"What the hell?"

"Crazy, isn't it? Cancers all over - in my kidneys, my brain, down in my guts; all over...but I beat 'em each time. It wasn't easy. I felt knackered after every bout but I kept fighting. I had to get back to the rig."

"What pushed you? After cancer four or five I'd have said 'fuck it' and mailed it in."

"I thought about it plenty of times but a lot kept me going. There was a book I read by Barnali Roy that talked about creating your own reality. She had some really interesting points, and since I was laid up and hooked up to machines, I didn't have a lot of other things to do but read. I combed through all the books in Binati and Helen's collection too. They've got some pretty awesome stuff in there, you know?

I read all kinds of stuff, man. Caroline's stuff about the power of imagination was mind-bending – like, really mind-bending. She's apparently some big shot Social Media guru from California, but this was next-level.

I also read Stephen Ericson's erotica. That one was really fun."

"A male erotica author?"

"Told you, mate. This ain't the same place you're from. Things run a bit differently here but yeah, he's great. His books are more than just the sex, it's about human potential. They are about finding the diamonds in everyone. For some reason, there's also a lot of oranges in there. In fact, if I remember correctly, one of the sex scenes used an orange to..."

"Ok, I get the picture. Tell me more about Barnali's book. What did you mean by the power of characters?"

"Well, she talked about how creating characters can help shape what's actually happening in your life, so I created the character of Darren the cancer-killer. Quite a badass, actually. The cancer was a bitch, man. I was as crook as Rookwood."

"Huh?"

"It means sick. You don't get out much, do you?"

Well, played, sir.

"But the book really helped. So did the paintings that Kelsey sent me."

"You know Kelsey?"

"Of course. Kelsey drew the illustrations of Darren the cancer-killer. It was awesome. It made me think he was real. Over time, he became real. He started kicking its ass left and right. Every single time the cancer came back, he jumped into action. Now, I'm back in this seat where I belong."

"I still can't believe you didn't give up."

"It occurred to me once or twice. You know *that fella* that keeps lurking around you? The weird, Shadowy guy?"

"I've crossed paths with him once or twice."

"Yeah. I never knew the bloke before the cancer. But then he showed up to my bed, and told me to come with him. He told me to pull out the plugs. He told me that the cancer that was just going to keep coming back again and again. He told me how I'd never sit in the seat of my rig after the cancer went through me. He told me how the cancer would just leave me as a pitiful bag of bones. Finally, he told me that I should spare myself the indignity by just coming with him and putting an end to it all."

"Sounds reasonable enough. What did you say to him?"

"I told him to get fucked."

"Wow. Ok. Then what?"

"Then he buggered off. Never saw him again."

Darren was the first person I'd ever met who told the Shadow to kiss his ass and get bent.

Maybe if the whole world were just Aussie truckers, we could have left 2020 in one fell swoop.

"Nah mate. My old lady can barely stand the one of me."

Fair.

After some time on the road...how long, I really couldn't tell you, the truck pulled into the parking lot of a sports bar.

"Where are we, man?"

"Still in Virginia."

"Huh?"

"What, did you think I was going to drive you to the moon or something?"

"Kind of, yeah."

"It's time for the games. They're expecting you."

"You coming with? After the road trip, you could probably use a bite, yeah?"

"I've got other business to tend to. Michelle's waiting for me back home."

So it was.

That was the last I saw of Darren.

He wasn't just a cancer-slayer. He was a Shadow-slayer.

Bad ass.

As the truck drove away, I saw a bumper sticker on it that said, "Viva la resistance".

Son of a bitch.

He was on board. I should have figured.

So we had…artists, lovebirds and a trucker? So far, it sounds more like a Village People cover band than a resistance against the scourge of all existence.

But, c'est la vie. I had to work with what I got.

You told me to go inside and take a seat in the middle of the bar, next to two middle-aged guys.

When I walked in, there were two people in the bar, both middle-aged guys.

I appreciate you at least making this part easy on me.

One of the guys was named Fitz, and the other Keith.

Fitz looked like your classic guy from the Midwest, at least what I'd seen in movies anyway. The wholesome American uncle you'd find at Thanksgiving, until he was a whiskey or two in and started talking politics.

Keith looked like a former football player; powerfully built, shiny bald head, and a megawatt smile.

"Hell of a game, isn't it?" said Fitz, pointing to the screen directly in front of us.

"We're going to take it to your boys today, Fitzie", said Keith.

It was a Michigan State-Iowa college football game.

I never knew much about college football. I just followed the NFL, and to keep up with my theme of self-hatred, I was a Jets fan.

"I'm sorry, man", said Keith, "I wouldn't wish that on anyone."

I appreciated the sympathy.

"But at least you guys have that fireman, right? The guy who leads the J-E-T-S chants and gets the crowd going nuts?"

"I wouldn't know. I've never been to a game."

"No? How about a Jets sports bar? Deck out in green and cheer for your boys with some friends?"

"Nope. I just used to have the games on at McCabe's in the corner with the sound off. I never really cared that much to get emotionally invested. It's just a bunch of millionaires who could care less if I lived or died."

"It's so much more than that", said Fitz, "It's about connection. Human connection."

"What's football got to do with connection?"

"Take a look at this game", said Keith, "I mean, really, take a look."

I looked. I saw two stagnant offenses.

"You know why the offense is stagnant for Michigan State? No connection. The quarterback is out for his stats, so he's trying to fit the ball into tight windows that don't exist. The running back thinks he's going in the first round, so his pretty little self doesn't want to break a nail by blocking anyone.

The wide receiver thinks he's also too big a deal to block anyone, so he lets the DB come crashing down. And the left tackle? He hates the quarterback. So, he's letting him get hit all day. He's not blocking for him at all."

"Ok? Still not picking up what you're putting down."

"Now look at the defense. Really look."

I saw sparks lighting up around Keith as he started talking about the defense. I saw those sparks lighting up around the defensive players too.

"Look at Marcus there, the middle linebacker. You don't know this, but Marcus saw his brother shot in front of him in high school. He almost followed the same path. The guy who hangs around and tries to kill your spirit, you know who I'm talking about...he got in Marcus's ear. Told him life was a waste and that nothing mattered. He almost listened to him too. But football lit him up. It got Marcus out of bed in the morning. It kept him out of trouble. Football kept him driven and motivated. It made him believe he could be something more. Now watch this."

I turned my eyes back up to the game, and I saw Marcus, number 50, lit up in sparks and lighting everyone else around him. I saw eleven guys, all working as one, moving as one, coming together and connecting on a subatomic level. I actually saw their vibrating energy patterns speaking to each other.

"You see?" said Keith, "He destroys us individually but together, connected, he can't touch us."

I think I know why you wanted me to see this. You wanted me to see connection outside the romantic setting in the winery.

That we meant more to each other than just a prosecco bath or other form of happily ever-after.

Fitz chimed in too.

"Keith played for Iowa. The game is very personal to him. But to me, everything around the game is what matters more."

"How so?"

"You see the town they're playing in? It's called East Lansing, Michigan. I came up there for the first time when I was in 6th grade. It was in a broken-down old bus, but my teacher really wanted us to see this place. I was from a small farm town and never thought I was smart enough to go to college. The people in my town never left and never saw much of the world. That's just how it was. We had blinders on to what was outside. But when I got there, for the first time, I felt like there was...more.

There were students sitting outside on blankets, eating, laughing, tossing the frisbee around. It was spring, so the flowers were in full

m. Everyone seemed happy. But more than that...they seemed...alive. Like, they were living the greatest years they would ever have in this place, and in the process, setting down roots that would connect them back to it forever. I graduated from here forty years ago, but I always come back."

"Why, still missing a credit or two from biology?"

"No man, for football. My buddies and I gather every year for Homecoming. Matt, Charlie, Ben, Brian, hell, even Andy. We set up a tailgate, talk crap to each other about how fat we got and how much hair we lost; throw some steaks and dogs on the grill, drink some cold ones from the cooler, let our wives commiserate about God-knows-what, and relive the old times. Then, we go into the stadium and scream our butts off for three hours."

"Got it. So that's cool. You've got a tradition. It connects you and your buddies."

"Not just my buddies. Look around. There are 76,000 people wearing the same colors, shouting the same lyrics to the same song, cheering for the same team. This level of connection is only possible through football."

"So...your connection isn't to the school, but to the football team?"

"The football team is just the conduit. The school is the spark. It lights us all up. We light each other up. Wait till you see it in action after we score our first touchdown."

Three and a half quarters went by, and there were no touchdowns.

"Yeah, well, our offense is putrid this year. It happens."

"I get it. Remember? Jets fan."

You at least seemed to be enjoying yourself watching the game. You really took it all in and were enamored by the crowd size and energy.

"To think, Sean, this almost didn't happen."

"How do you mean?"

"He tried to get this all shut down forever."

Of course I knew who he was talking about.

"He doesn't have that power. How could he?"

"He got in the ear of the power brokers and told them that shutting this down forever was the only safe thing to do. No more football wouldn't matter, it was just a small price to pay to be safe. To think that they almost listened to him."

"What ended up happening?"

"Look at the game, buddy. He lost. The people spoke. We weren't going to let these sparks be extinguished. Other tribes spoke up in the same way. We fought to keep our sparks alive. We fought to keep this connection alive. We did all this because every time another brat gets thrown on the grill, every time two old farts give each other a hug, every time we hear that fight song, something inside us gets lit up. Those sparks fly. They connect us with all the others. The millions of Spartans around the world are lit up in unison."

"Spartans?"

"That's what we call ourselves. Michigan State Spartans."

"Who are your rivals? The Athenians?"

"You mean pompous asses who think they're smarter than everyone?"

"Yeah."

"Yep...we have a rival like that."

"Well, congrats on not losing these connections. Looks like it means a lot to you Spartans."

"It does. Tell me, did you ever play a sport?"

"I played a semester of high school basketball."

"Were you any good?"

"Coach said I had the silkiest-smooth jump shot he'd ever seen."

"So why only a semester?"

"Well...I was talked into quitting."

"By him."

"Yeah. He told me I was wasting my time. He said I wasn't big enough to play college ball anyway, so what was the point? He always planted these thoughts in my mind about getting permanently injured playing and ending up as some kind of an invalid. I of course listened."

"I'm sorry to hear that. Did you at least have the college experience?"

"One semester at Junior College. If you want to call that an experience."

"Let me guess, same talkin' to about quitting?"

"Same."

Talking to Fitz and Keith drove something home for me.

I left so much on the table. There was so much to be discovered, explored and experienced.

I could have been connected to my teammates on the court had I stayed in the game and on the team. I'd probably still be friends with them today and be invited to their kid's boring birthday parties in the suburbs. Their wives would try to fix me up with their annoying friends. There would probably be lots of wine and cheese and people in sweaters. It would be amazing, actually.

Had I gone to college, I could have been a part of one of these tribes Fitz was talking about. A Spartan or an Athenian, or whatever the hell they were. I could have made friends there too. I would have felt a sense of tradition when my team played. I could have felt a level of connection and camaraderie with other alumni.

"Beating yourself up again, are you? Hmm...this isn't good. You know this isn't good!" said a voice next to me, a voice that was near and dear to me.

Shanthi. It was my dear friend Shanthi.

"Shanthi! I didn't expect to see you here!"

I was overcome with a warm glow. Fitz and Keith were great guys to hang with, but Shanthi was always a sight for sore eyes.

"Of course I came, Sean! Did you know, this is one of Ritvik's new restaurants?"

"What? Ritvik has a sports bar in Virginia?"

"Of course. His food is everywhere. You must have the tamarind fries. You will be very pleased."

Again with the food; never change, Shanthi.

But I was so happy to see her. I wondered what became of her after I left the living room.

"Sean, I know you're replaying all the scenes of your life in your mind. You're watching a movie of yourself. I know it. I feel it. You mustn't do this, you know? It's not good."

"But I really messed things up. I dug my own grave and gave him every opening to come and get me. I could have done so many things to fight him off. I could have been better positioned to weather this storm. I could have left 2020 without jumping the way I did."

"You cannot look backwards. Only look forward. Your story only goes in one direction. This direction must point to a place of acceptance."

"How?"

"You will soon find out. But remember to keep your heart open, just like the Mermaid did. She is now on a very important mission."

"Let me guess, you can't tell me, but I'll soon find out?"

"You're so funny!" she laughed.

"But also correct. You will find out soon. But not now. This is about you now."

"Can you both keep it down? The game's about to start!" yelled Mel, who was sitting right next to her.

Well I'll be damned.

"Here", she said, as she slid a napkin over to me, "Notice anything?"

I saw a piece of artwork on the napkin.

"She really crushed it, didn't she?"

"Who really crushed it?"

"Look closer."

The napkin had a logo on it, as did all the napkins in the place.

It was a logo of a sacred spiral.

How do you like that!

"I knew Ana-Maria and Kelsey had it in them", said Mel, "The art is spreading. The connection is spreading."

"How do you think they did it?

"You know how. They wanted it. Everyone, everywhere...they wanted this. They're trapped in 2020 and desperate to leave. He's trying to keep them stuck there but the spiral spoke to them. It let them know there was more to do - an infinite canvass of possibilities."

As Mel said this, the bar slowly started filling up. British football fans and Indian cricket fans were filling in everywhere. They were all wearing the logo of the spiral on their jerseys.

"The logo's artwork reached one of them, who then reached out to the rest", said Mel, "The lockdowns kept them shuttered inside but the spiral helped them find each other again. Kelsey designed it and Ana-Maria shared it with them."

I saw a large group of Chelsea and Liverpool fans descend on our area of the bar.

"Careful with them", said Mel, "Especially the Liverpool ones. They can be a bit much."

"Oh, I wouldn't worry about them", said Fitz, "Have you ever seen a group of Ohio State fans?"

No one seemed to know what the other was talking about, but we all had a good laugh about it.

The Liverpool fans gathered near us at the bar, ordered a few pitchers, poured themselves a pint, connected with one another by putting their arms around each other's shoulders, and started singing their team song, "You'll never walk alone".

When you walk through a storm,

Hold your head up high,

And don't be afraid of the dark,

At the end of a storm,

There's a golden sky,

And the sweet silver song of a lark.

Walk on through the wind,

Walk on through the rain,

Though your dreams be tossed and blown,

Walk on, walk on, with hope in your heart,

And you'll never walk alone,

You'll never walk alone.

Fitz got a tear in his eye watching this.

"This is how it feels when me and my friends would get together and sing MSU Shadows", he said, "Not to be confused with, you know...*him*. It a song about our alma mater. But more so, it is a song about us, who we are, what we've experienced together. It is a song about what brought us as individuals together to form one big, green family. He could never touch us during that song."

Try as he might, he couldn't touch those Liverpool fans now. Each of them was exploding with sparks as they toasted their pints and belted that song at the top of their lungs.

It was the resistance in its purest form. It was a bold and proud middle finger to the Shadow.

Shanthi then said, "Look, at the end of the bar. I want you to see this too. I defied the lockdown to go to the market to get some more garlic…"

"You're the most badass rebel of them all, Shanthi."

"I know that. But when I arrived, I saw a chutney display arranged in a spiral. I thought it was highly peculiar. Then I remembered the ancient texts I read about. There's a meaning to this. Oh my, I thought, this is important! I must tell someone. So, I elbowed the man next to me, and told him this was our ticket to freedom. That this spiral would free us up from 2020. And he must tell everyone."

"What did he say?"

"He said something very unpleasant to me in Tamil about me being a crazy woman or something. But his friend next to him understood the message and he spread the word around Chennai. Look at these men who have arrived!"

There were a group of about a dozen Indian guys wearing yellow Chennai Super Kings Jerseys. Apparently, this is a really big-time cricket team in India.

"They are Chennai, and Chennai is them", said Shanthi.

In unison, they started whistling, which was the precursor to them breaking out into the "Whistle Podu" song.

They started whistling and dancing and going crazy. It was amazing. I never saw anything like this at McCabe's with the borderline-suicidal Jets fans.

"You see", said Shanthi, "This is what he cannot defeat."

Mel suddenly became very dour.

I asked her what was wrong.

"It hurts to see this."

"Why? This is great. This is exactly how we fight him."

"Yes, but it reminds me of the conventions. We used to have moments like this. People dressed as Wookies doing karaoke, Klingons having bat'leth battle demonstrations. It was absolutely magical. Perfection. This just reminds me how that it's all gone."

"Mel", said Shanthi, "You've come such a long way. You will still have moments like this. Moments of joy and moments of sadness. It's completely normal to feel this way. Don't worry! Your time will come. I too look upon this with some sadness in my heart. My babies should have been here to see this with me, to see the spirit of Chennai rise in defiance of him. They should be here to see us rise in defiance of the bolting down of our souls. But you're here, and so are you, Sean. That is more than enough. Chennai now lives through you as well."

I guess I was now a cricket fan.

"Football fan too, mate." said one of the Liverpool guys.

"Come on, now. Don't go calling that thing football", said Keith.

I've never seen a "football" vs. "football" pissing match before. It was pretty great.

One thing though was abundantly clear to me - connection through sports, through these tribes, was as potent as anything I'd ever witnessed.

It broke down all kinds of barriers between people. The Liverpool fans were from different socio-economic backgrounds, but that song united them all. The Chennai fans were brought together through the fault lines of religion, caste and all the other things they overwise squabble over on a daily basis.

Keith and Fitz grew up very differently. Fitz grew up in a small, rural town in the Midwest and Keith in the urban toughness of New Jersey. Yet, college football brought them together.

What had I been missing all this time?

Was this the key?

Was I the one meant to bring together sports fans all over the world to fight him?

"Ah shit, now you've done it", said Mel.

"Done what?"

"Gone all messianic and self-important. Sarah's going to have to slap you back to reality a bit."

"Who?"

"So...the savior of all creation doesn't even know me? Bit of a half-assed savior you are, if I say so myself" said this strawberry blonde British woman standing behind me.

"This connection is all well and good.", she said, "Might even give you a bit of meaning or something. But you've already become a part of the resistance, yeah? Or you too drunk to realize it?"

I had no idea who she was, nor what she was talking about.

"Ever rode on an elephant while drinking Amaretto?", she asked.

Can't say I have!

I could see Irish Pete trying to pull some shit like that after a number of rounds.

"I've seen it many times at weddings in Chennai" said Shanthi.

True.

"But have you seen an elephant drinking Amaretto too?" asked Sarah.

No one seemed to have a yes answer for that.

"Come on then. Maybe you'll learn a little something, shed that Jesus complex you've got and get on with the next part of this little adventure of yours, yeah?"

You laughed and told me to go with Sarah.

I looked over at Fitz and Keith.

"You guys good?"

"Better than good. We've got football back, man", said Keith, "but you need to go with Sarah. We'll be here if you need us. And we know the Mermaid's got our back too."

"The Mermaid is tied into this?"

"Absolutely", said Fitz, "She's tied into everything. Go Green!"

As I was leaving, I wanted to say goodbye to Shanthi and Mel, but didn't. Something held me back. I just couldn't at the moment.

"Go on", said Mel, "I'll be fine. I just need to let this one pass."

I was worried about her, but deep down I knew she'd be ok. Somehow, I was certain I would see her again. That much I knew beyond the shadow of a doubt.

No pun.

But for now, Sarah needed to bust my balls and cut me down to size. I was up for that.

So were you, as always.

Chapter 10: Elephants and Amaretto

"Ok Sean, maybe we do this before all matter implodes and the universe ends? That might be a trifle convenient. Don't want to put you out or anything. It's up to you", said Sarah.

I appreciated the razzing. Always had.

You once again opened a vortex for us to travel through.

Sarah went first, and said, "This vortex thing better not ruin my white pants. I quite like these."

In fairness, they were really solid white pants.

This vortex, unlike the others, moved really quickly and in a blink, we were spit out onto a wide-open plain in Africa.

It looked like something I'd once seen in a documentary about the Serengeti.

I was in Tanzania? Kenya? Somewhere around there.

It was stunning.

Open grassland and Acacia trees as far as the eye could see. Rock formations in the distance, with a stiff breeze blowing through under a clear blue sky and powerful beating sun.

Also, there were elephants. My God, were there elephants! Everywhere. There must have been two dozen of them within eyeshot.

"Told you there'd be elephants", said Sarah, who appeared next to me, "Watch this."

She had a massive, gallon-sized bottle of Amaretto handy, and walked up to the elephant in the lead of the pack.

"Thanks, sis", the elephant said, as it dipped its trunk in to take a swig.

Ok, what?

We're onto talking elephants now?

"Let's go, Sean. Even you're capable of riding one of these things for 10 seconds without falling off."

I wish Mel were there at the moment.

She would have chimed in with a perfect, "That's what she said."

Sarah climbed onto the lead elephant, and I climbed onto the one next to her.

She tossed me a small bottle of Amaretto so I could enjoy it along with her, and the talking elephant.

"Hey, Mr. Elephant", she said to her ride, "No cracks about me putting on weight during lockdown, got it?"

"Nah, you look great", he said, "I'm an expert in this department. I haven't been able to fit into my summer tusk in years."

Yeah.

This wasn't strange…at all.

Alongside us, we saw another rider on an elephant.

It was Edna.

"Hey you two! Glad you waited for me to catch up. I rode all the way down from Nairobi."

"Is that far from here?" I wondered. Kenyan geography wasn't my strong suit.

"It's pretty far on an elephant!"

"Great, well, glad you joined us. What brought you down from the city?"

"I had to escape. He almost got me. I was very close. He had me right where he wanted me. But I knew something was waiting for me down here, so I left."

"I'm assuming you're talking about *who* I think you're talking about."

"Of course. I don't speak his name though, or I find myself right back in the cage."

"The *cage*?"

Shit. This sounded ominous. I'd read in the news about some bad stuff going down in East Africa.

"Yes. The cubicle I worked in."

Phew. Ok. I could work with this.

"You see, corporate life in Kenya is very demanding. There is intense pressure to succeed. We have to bring honor to our family, to our tribe and to ourselves. That cubicle, to me, was a cage. Every day, my jailor would look over my shoulder and tell me what I could and could not do, what I could and could not think, and controlled every aspect of my being."

"Sounds like hell", said Sarah, "Did you at least have any Amaretto?"

We both gave Sarah a glare.

"Alright then, as you were."

"You see, Sean, Sarah...it was more than simply a cage. It was a, for want of a better word...a "path" for my soul's final ending. I am always bursting with energy, with thoughts of other places, of other possibilities, of this big playground of creation where we can do whatever we want. And yet, in this cage, I was forbidden to do anything. I needed to show up at a certain time, do one thing, make my overseer happy, then return home. There was no freedom. There was no laughter. There was no creativity. There was nothing. Every day, I felt more and more of the light leaving me."

"So what made you finally leave?", I wondered.

"I knew you both would be here. I had a vision of two women…a redhead and another with green eyes. They were two kindred spirits. They told me to find you here. They told me how there were these people from other places who would roam the Serengeti freely with me, freely with these wonderful beasts of creation…people who don't see reality the same as the others."

"What do you mean? How do the others see it?"

"The others see rigidity. They see rules. Rules of physics, rules of nature, rules of behavior. You two mock these rules. You ridicule them. You see the preposterous nature of such confines. You play outside of these rules with your snarky and witty commentary. To you both, it's sarcasm. But you don't quite understand the power of what you're accomplishing."

"Please, enlighten us, Obi-Wan", said Sarah.

"By not taking the rules seriously, you open the doorway to new avenues of thought. You take the dancing particles of all we've created and make them dance even more. You make them more playful. You make it more likely to lead to other possibilities. Take these elephants for instance."

"What about them?"

"Who's ever heard of an Amaretto-drinking elephant who speaks and has a self-deprecating sense of humor?"

"Probably only us."

"Exactly. But you have the power to share this vision with others. The irreverence of this place is something that has more potency than you can hope to understand. It's an unraveling of the rules that lead everyone to him. A dismantling of the structures that say an elephant cannot speak, and has no taste for a coffee liquor. Those structures are what convince others that possibilities don't exist. That all we see…is ordinary. But there's more. We're bound only by the limits of our imagination."

As Edna was speaking, you gave me a look that said, "I know this sounds nuts but this is really important and you need to pay attention."

"You see, Sarah, by you, as you call it, 'taking the piss' out of people, you're actually destroying their rigid pathways. You're reducing what they see as concrete fortification of their hopeless story into nothing but a joke. You're releasing their pressure valves. You're freeing them from their cages."

"By mocking their stupid Welsh accents and self-important posts on social media and all the Mermaid's hippy shit?"

"Yes! Because they wrap up their identity in such things. If the post doesn't go viral, they start questioning why they're a failure in life. Then he shows up to reinforce that belief. It's the little failures of things we take seriously that he feeds on. He knows when to strike. He always knows when to strike. But when you show up to destroy such thoughts with humor, he has no power. He cannot build a path when one is laughing, because the light of laughter negates the very existence of the path."

"What about comedians? They're the most depressed bastards out there!"

"Of course they are, and comedy is their weapon to fight him. The irreverence and mocking of these rules are the only weapons in their arsenal. But it helps others too."

"I'm no bloody comedian, that's for sure, Edna."

"You don't have to be. You only need to be Sarah. You need to keep creating talking elephants who enjoy Amaretto as much as you do."

"Damn right I do!", said the Elephant that Sarah was riding, with a noticeably slurred speech and more of a wobble in its step.

"Alright, let me off, you drunken knob!" she yelled.

Sarah dismounted from the elephant, and as soon as she hit the ground, the elephant passed out and started drooling.

"You ok, bro?", I asked, fully expecting a response.

The elephant slowly nodded its head before passing out again.

Good. Let it sleep it off. Calling it an Uber out here would be a real bitch anyway.

Shortly after the elephant passed out, another one rode up, this time with Alysandra as its passenger.

"Wow, that took forever", she said.

"Tell me - where do you come from?" said Edna.

"Singapore. So yeah, this was a really long ride. I'm sore."

"That really is a long frickin' ride", I injected.

"Don't I know it!", said Alysandra's elephant, "The whole time we were discussing bio-engineered humans, aliens and spies!"

"That sounds like a pretty good way to pass the time. What did you guys come up with?"

"Well, we concluded that aliens are real, and happened to bio-engineer humans that then turned into spies."

"That seems like a lazy way to piece it all together if I'm just being honest."

"Yeah," said Sarah, "I'd expect this type of tripe from one of Bruce's trending posts, but not from an elephant who had a few months to discuss this with someone from Singapore."

"You guys are brutal!" said Alysandra.

"They have their moments", said Edna.

We were roasting an elephant. Awesome. All we needed was a dais table and Dean Martin to host.

Something about all this felt very, for lack of a better word, natural.

It all flowed really easily. There was no resistance.

Despite how utterly preposterous this all was, none of us really batted an eyelash at any of it. The ridiculousness was as 'real' as anything any one of us has ever experienced.

Hard-drinking, talking elephants who opined about spies and aliens were simply another manifestation of creation…something we all cobbled up together. That makes all this as real as my building on the Lower East Side or the piles of trash that lay alongside it.

"Sean", said Edna, "Remember the wrestling? You've forgotten. Life made you forget. But try to remember, please? Because that broke you out of your cage too."

The wrestling? What was she talking about?

Wrestling?

The...oh.

Right.

The wrestling "federation" we had when I was in high school. The *XRWA* or the "Extreme Raw Wrestling Association." God, that was a hoot.

Me and some of the old crew used to get together behind the building on Avenue B, in the grassy area between our building and the next one, and utterly kick the shit out of each other.

We loved wrestling. This was in the early 2000s when it was still a pretty big thing.

It was a great outlet for our aggression, especially since none of us were man enough to go up against the really tough characters in the neighborhood.

Yes, not even Cortez. He talked a big game but would shit his pants when a real Latin King showed up.

Wrestling was our way of creating something. It was a way of letting our irreverence fly.

It wasn't about the wrestling itself; it was about the creativity around it. We created characters and storylines around the wrestling.

Cortez was "King Cortez", who'd walk into the ring wearing a massive knock-off crown he bought for five bucks in Chinatown.

Irish Pete would then be announced as his opponent, and he would walk into the ring to the sound of Irish fiddling music, draped in an Irish flag, wearing a leprechaun hat.

It was as stupid as it was amazing.

There were others too. Richie was Richie Rich, who would come in with bling all over him and toss Monopoly money all over the place.

I should have known something was wrong with Rich once he stopped coming out. He loved that character and hitting Cortez over the head with a chair.

In fairness, everyone loved hitting Cortez over the head with a chair.

But once Rich stopped coming out, that's when the Shadow got him. That's when he took him down a path he never came back from. Looking back on it now, Rich was the safest when he was being power-bombed into a flaming, barbed-wire table.

Perhaps more chair-shots to the face and German suplexes into the ground would have been the best thing for him because while we were together, he wasn't able to get his claws into any of us. We were free, and we were light. We were, as they said in the Shawshank Redemption, "The Lords of all creation."

Nothing was able to penetrate that wall we put up. In retrospect, it was a bright wall of light. This light comprised of callout interviews when we said things like, "...and I'm here to tell King Candyass; when I get you in the ring next week, I'm going to send you home in a body bag! Yeaaahhhh!!!!"

In our own peculiar way, that was our expression of irreverence, of creation, and of life.

It was our way of fighting for what was ours, and what we had the capacity to imagine.

We even developed a small following in the neighborhood, with kids who used to come out and cheer on their favorite characters.

These were poor kids like us from the projects. They didn't have shit and neither did we.

A lot of them came from fucked-up homes with abusive relatives, drugs and God-knows-what-else.

But for a fleeting moment during the weekends, we allowed their imaginations to run wild. We allowed them to believe in possibilities. We allowed their light to shine and mingle with ours. Our performances and their cheering lit each other's sparks.

...and I never realized it while it was happening. Not for a second. But looking back, I should have.

Frankie Marabucci, a Sicilian kid, decided to play the role of "Frankie the Frenchie". He'd strut into the ring with French accordion music playing, carrying a loaf of bread and twirling his fake mustache. He was a fan favorite. He'd step into the ring and yell, "Viva la resistance!", and all the neighborhood kids would shout it with him.

"Viva la resistance!"

Son of a bitch.

Frankie, you sly devil; you pasta-eating, freedom-fighting, Shadow-slaying bastard, you.

He knew it all along. He knew what we were doing. He knew why we were doing it...and he knew for whom we were doing it.

It never occurred to the rest of us consciously but something was propelling us to leave our apartments, come out into that grassy patch and beat the living dogshit out of each other to the cheering sounds of dangerously unsupervised children.

We were the resistance.

I thought I was in his grip my entire life.

But turns out I'd been fighting the bastard for as long as I can remember.

He won plenty of bouts, more than his share - talking me out of basketball, college, a life with Sam and a possibility with Tess.

Now I know though...I fought back. I just never realized it.

"You see", said Edna, "This isn't a new journey for you. This is a continuation. Your friend Frank broke out of his cage with his character. As did your friend Cortez. As did you, and as will you once more."

"So what now? It's great that I've already been fighting this...but it still led me here. It wasn't enough apparently."

"The fight is not meant to be won. It's meant to be fought."

Wait...WHAT?

"She's right", said Brian, who came riding up in an elephant of his own.

Elephants seemed to be the Teslas of this part of the universe.

Brian was a guy from Cincinnati, with glasses and a quiet confidence that suggested he did some real bad-ass things that he otherwise doesn't like talking about in mixed company.

"Have you ever played hopscotch?"

"What?"

"Hopscotch. You know, the game where you hop around like bunnies."

"I saw the girls in my school play it outside. Why? What does hopscotch have to do with anything?"

I was getting a little agitated with the hopscotch talk, because I couldn't shake what Edna has just said to me.

Fighting him was not to win, but to just fight?

Was all this for nothing?

"Hopscotch is like life", said Brian, "and a lot like war. Trust me, I know a lot about war. I was in the Marine Corps. I've seen things that'll curdle your skin hundred times over. *That demon,* you know the *guy,* tried getting his claws into me multiple times. He unfortunately got his claws into many of my brothers who served with me. We lost more when we got home to him, more than we lost on the frontlines. It was hopscotch which saved me."

"Going to need more than this, man."

"Think of it this way, what can PTSD do in the face of hopscotch? What can existential dread wreak upon you in the face of hopscotch? Nothing. You simply hop. All your energy is diverted from him. You hop, and you jump, and you yell things. It's great."

"Yeah... and when you're tired and sit down, then he gets you."

"Yep. And then we fuel up and hop again. It's a lot like a guerilla war. It's each side exchanging hit and runs. Each attacking the other in their weak spots. There are no clear winners and losers. You fight to win. But winning means not losing. It doesn't mean actually winning. Some wars just can't be won."

I really wasn't happy now. This sounded too defeatist for me.

I came all this way, and now I'm being told it's a waste? There is really no beating him?

Why did Binati and Helen send me on this mission then?

Why was he so threatened by Ana-Maria and Kelsey?

No... this didn't add up.

Battles don't go on forever. There are no endless wars. These wars just feel endless.

There had to be something I was missing.

Either we can beat this guy or we can't. But once again, I needed answers.

My elephant simply said, "Hop on. Let's go get those answers."

Wherever he was taking me, I suspected things would become clearer.

"Don't worry, I'll see you again", said Edna, "The Mermaid has made sure of it."

"Yep", said Sarah, "She's really on a roll with that hippie shit."

So the elephant and I both took a swig of Amaretto and hit the road.

Chapter 11: BBQ and Corn

Have you ever had a long, interesting discussion with an elephant?

Of course you haven't.

What a ridiculous question.

No one has.

Except maybe Sarah, Edna, Alysandra and Brian.

Nevertheless, even though I know you may not remember, you were there to witness it all.

It was really something.

This elephant knew a lot about a lot. We both agreed that the Jack Nicholson *Joker* was far superior to the rendition played by Heath Ledger, which I always thought was a minority opinion.

But apparently, it's a widely shared belief in the greater talking elephant community, so that was a relief.

The elephant was especially chatty about other travelers he met along the way. He was going on about someone named Liz, who rode him for over a month while touring Southeast Asia.

Liz was bubbly and chatty, and asked the elephant about all sorts of things. He really enjoyed spending time with Liz and talked about the sparks that she emitted when she discussed her love of traveling.

He said that traveling lit the sparks of everyone he came across. Something about exploring new places, meeting new people, and eating new foods, even ones that made them sick, seemed to light everyone all up.

It reminded me again that I hadn't ever really been anywhere. But before I found myself falling into a spiral where he would show up, I remembered what Violeta told me at the winery, "Your story was still to be written, Sean."

Maybe if I ever got back, I could go somewhere.

Anywhere.

Even Buffalo.

After many moons riding this elephant, it dropped me off at a BBQ restaurant in Raleigh, North Carolina.

"Well, this is where we part", he said.

"Thanks for the lift. I'll never forget you."

"I know you won't. Long live Jack Nicholson."

"Indeed, my friend. Long live Jack."

He turned and began the long journey back, with a "Viva la resistance" tattoo on his backside.

My man.

I waited for half an hour outside the restaurant, intuitively feeling that I was supposed to meet someone here.

But riding an elephant across time and space also works up a pretty healthy appetite, so I went in and got myself some slaw and hush puppies to pass the time.

I wish they had places like this on the Lower East Side. Cortez especially would've loved this joint. That guy's a bottomless pit.

I started to dig in, and while I was waiting for my BBQ sandwich to be brought to me, I heard, "Sean, there you are!"

It was Sabriya, and she burst through the doors, ran up to my table and gave me a huge hug.

"Umm...hey?"

"I'm so joyful to see you here. I love this place. It always lights me up. Try the pulled pork sandwich with extra vinegar, trust me."

She must've read my mind because that's exactly what I ordered. But since she already knew my name in a place that was in some nebulous realm between life and death, it stood to reason she'd know my order too.

Sabriya and I grabbed a table near the back, with all the fixings - the sauce, the sauce, and, well, the sauce.

I wish you'd decided to eat with us. You really missed out.

"Have you tried the new sauce?" she asked.

"Which one?"

"The one from Chef Agrawal in India! The chef that Shanthi loves! It's a curry BBQ creation. He adapted it just for Carolina. It's amazing! I had it for the first time with Greg and Judy when they drove through here on their way to Sue Singh's winery last time."

She was name-dropping characters from this journey like a boss.

"I love Greg and Judy, don't you?"

"I do, Sabriya. They really are the best."

"Did they tell you about the prosecco and what they do when..."

"Yeah, I cut them off. Some things are better left unsaid."

She chuckled a bit then got to her sandwich.

One thing that was peculiar about Sabriya that was different from all the rest… she had subtle sparks flying around her from the minute she walked in.

Others had them situationally, after a big embrace or talking about something that lit them up.

I saw them in Shanthi's living room.

I saw them when Judy and Greg were talking about breaking each other free from the Witch and the Wizard.

I saw them when Fitz was describing his gameday tailgates with his buddies.

But Sabriya had what can only be described as "perma-spark."

I asked her about it. I suspected this was central to why I needed to meet her.

Again, I watch enough movies; Chekov's gun and all. This wasn't happening by accident.

"I wasn't always like this", she said, "Joy didn't always come naturally to me. For much of my life, I had to keep my head down and mouth shut. Growing up in the South, there are things that happen that you just keep quiet about. We never had these talks with my parents.

But when I got to college, I saw a noose fastened off the highway underpass with racial slurs scribbled next to it. I was horrified beyond words. I always suspected I'd encounter something like this as a Black woman at some point in my life, but nothing can really prepare you for it when it happens."

I was waiting for her sparks to disappear and for him to show up. This was usually his opening. He existed for moments like this, like a vulture.

But nothing changed. Her sparks got even brighter and more intense.

"And believe me when I say...I saw and experienced much worse than that too. But I don't need to tell you, Sean. You already know my story."

"No... keep going. I know it...but I need to hear it."

"The night of the noose incident, I went home and cried. I cried at the kind of cruelty that lived in people's hearts. I cried that I could be seen as less than human by someone who never even met me. But more than anything...I cried at those who would see it and be less equipped to handle it than me. Those who would see it...then succumb to him and start believing his narrative that this life wasn't worth living."

"Go on."

"I knew that whoever put that up was inspired by him. They put that up there with the sole purpose of demonstrating the flaws of what we've built together here; to drive separation and disconnection, to harden hearts, to turn us against each other, and drive each of us to him. So, on that day, I made it my mission to fight him."

"With what?"

"With radical joy."

"Sounds like name of a Chinese baking product."

"I know, right?!? But I like it anyway. I started hosting retreats to facilitate this radical joy. There are a dozen happening concurrently right now."

"How? You're here?"

"My radical joy ambassadors hold it down. They're each carrying a spark of me, which is carrying a spark of everything."

"How do you facilitate radical joy? No offense, but it sounds kinda fluffy and not particularly concrete."

"You'll find out."

"I will?"

"Yes. In time. Just know that we create joy from pain. We don't hide from him. We acknowledge him and move forward together."

Her sparks were going crazy now. Not surprisingly, he was nowhere to be found. It was way too bright in here for his taste...and if I were to guess, he was probably more of a Kansas City BBQ guy.

"So, when you say acknowledge...help me out on this one. How can you both fight something and acknowledge it simultaneously? You beat him or you don't, right?"

"No, we're not going to beat him. He's not going anywhere. He'll always be there. There will always be another noose. There will always be another veteran who commits suicide. There will always be another abuse victim who can't make it one more day. But we're here to live *with* him. We are not here to deny he exists."

"What's the point then? What's the point of the endless fight?"

"Don't you see? It's always been an endless fight. We created this all together. This is ours. It took work. It still takes work. This is our baby. We're its parents...You know what Sean? Parents always fight for their babies, even in a world fraught with danger."

"What does *this* mean? What's our baby?"

"Everything. Our baby is literally everything. I'm helping my baby leave 2020."

It occurred to me in that moment why Sabriya was sparking continuously.

The other sparks she lit were lighting others, which were lighting others.

She lit the match on the dry tinder, and it was a wildfire ready to explode.

She lit the world around her.

A world in desperate need of joy.

A world that had been in his grip for far too long.

A world of people trapped in their tunnels of lockdowns, fear, anxiety, disconnection, hopelessness, and just begging to break out.

"There are others too", she said.

"Others who do what?"

"Who've turned a close brush with him into self-sustaining spark wildfires. Who don't fight him for a minute, but put enough light out there to fight him in perpetuity!"

The Shadow made a point of mocking my friends in Shanthi's living room.

He warned me about how their moment couldn't last. But I don't think he was counting on this - Self-sustaining spark machines that could keep him at bay for countless people.

This was something that never would have been possible before the age of the internet, where the whole world could be connected in a blink.

In the past, he could trap someone in the Kingdom of Mali or Prussia in their tunnels, and if everyone in their close circle around them was also trapped, they'd be his.

Now though, someone in Ghana, someone in Canada, someone in Dubai was just a click away from Sabriya. One click away from joy.

Of course he chose 2020 as his time to strike.

He couldn't wait any longer.

We were at a tipping point where the Sabriyas of the world could facilitate connections unlike anything remotely fathomable in the annals of human history.

I just had so many thoughts to ponder over as I wolfed down this BBQ while getting sauce all over my face.

"Sabriya, who are the others you're talking about?"

"There are so many. More than you'll ever encounter. There's Carolynn, who was utterly broken by 2020. She lost everything. She lost her job, her home, her friends and her self-respect. She relocated to California and didn't know a soul. Everything she'd taken for granted in her life was ripped away from her in an instant. She fell into his orbit, as you would expect...but she fought back. She allowed the light to break through and show her another possibility. Carolynn started a company for event professionals who've also been devastated by 2020, and she connects them to all types of different sparks and perspectives around the world. It's inclusivity in its purest form. It is allowing everything in. It is allowing everyone to have a voice. It is allowing everyone to continue their work; to continue building and to continue creating.

Her sparks are now everywhere. So are David's.

David had a stroke and thought that was the end. The Shadow visited him many times in the aftermath. He tried to convince him that this was the end, and that life in a compromised body no longer had any meaning. He whispered how this stroke was a fundamental example of a malicious creation that needed to, in his words, 'be brought to justice'. According to him, there was only one way to do that. But David fought back too. He fully recovered, and now he coaches people the world over to connect with their own light. He uses the principles of tai-chi to understand the connectedness of it all, and that his stroke was a turn, rather than a dead-end.

...and there are more, Sean. So, so many more."

This felt like a Tony Robbins seminar if ever saw one.

"Who else? Who do I need to find?"

"There's Paige too. Like me, and like the others, Paige is also helping people leave 2020. She started a company to help people move on from breakups and divorces. You know how many people split up this year because of all this? The numbers are crazy! But Paige is helping them heal, helping them rebuild. She is doing this one spark at a time. You should see this girl! She has perma-sparks around her, just like me; just radiating them in every direction. Margaret is like that too! How could I forget Margaret! She's in Nigeria but she's bringing people together all over as an event host! Birthdays, anniversaries, you name it! She won't let their joy die either."

"How do you know all these people?"

"The Mermaid. I know them all through the Mermaid."

Whatever mission the Mermaid had undertaken, it was clearly working. They all seemed to know her.

It also seemed as if Ana-Maria was fulfilling her purpose too. So was Kelsey.

Before I could get into another one of my self-pitying spirals about my own lack of accomplishment, Sabriya handed me a book.

"Here", she said, "I want you to read something."

She slid it across the table towards me.

"I think you'll enjoy this."

It was from an author named Carina Krehl, titled, "Thank you, Dammit". You'd expect me to say "Thank you, dammit" sarcastically when I'd get the electric bill in the mail. But this book was a metaphysical journey through 2020, told in Carina's words, through her own experiences, through her own unique perspective.

The Shadow often talked about perceptions, and how this is all one big perception, so I wondered, how different could her perception be from mine?

Were we all experiencing this thing the same way?

I couldn't wait to read it. Maybe it would open my eyes to something new; something that could help piece this all together.

I mean, I'd learned plenty so far.

I'd learned about the nature of the Shadow, about connection, love and creativity, and how they were all his kryptonite.

I'd learned about why I ended up here after I jumped.

I'd learned about why Mel ended up here after the pills.

Above all else, I learned about how leaving 2020 was more of a state of perception, rather than a physical time and place.

...which is why all these other people who didn't commit suicide were somehow here too.

I thanked Sabriya for the book, and asked if she would officially join the resistance.

I slid her a napkin I had with the spiral logo as a way of extending an official invitation.

She would be quite the asset for us.

"There's nothing to join", she said, "There's nothing to begin…only to continue."

Great.

Binati, what did you do to me?

Why did you send me on this wild goose chase just to meet people who are already doing their thing, and aren't going to be talked into anything more formal?

I thought I was some kind of a key to all this?

I asked you the same.

What was the end-game of all this?

Wasn't I suppose to corral them into one unified front? If not to defeat him, then to at least resist him together? Wasn't this united front supposed to be put up so we could all leave 2020 as a team?

It seemed that everyone was just doing their own thing. They all had resigned themselves to the fact that he wasn't going to be beaten, just fought in their own unique ways.

It could be through a piece of art, or a kiss, or singing at a football game.

Sabriya sensed the angst in me, and reassured me that everything was working out exactly as it needed to. Like the others, she also told me that we would meet again.

She gave me another big hug, then left.

The moment she walked out of the room though, I immediately felt the energy shift.

As per the custom, he appeared in the booth right across from me.

"She's been a thorn in my side longer than you'll ever know", he said, "but that's ok. She can't do this forever."

"I think you underestimate her."

"I know her better than you think. I know her like I know you."

"And what is it that you know, exactly?"

"That the minute your connections to each other fray, you're powerless against me. The void encircles you. The truth returns. You can attend your seminars. Your retreats. You can laugh. You can smile. You can hug. You can even do it virtually. You can inspire others. You can feel your sense of oneness and even delude yourselves into believing that this is the way to defeat me once and for all. But you know the truth, and so does she. Once the party is over, once you turn your devices off, once the football games are over, and once the stillness overcomes you, it's just me. It's always me. Your terror swallows you whole. And you come to me for answers. For certainty. For a path."

I had a sinking feeling in my stomach.

The bastard was right.

I thought about the wrestling matches, and how fun they were. The laughs, the camaraderie, and the flaming barbed-wire table that tore up Anthony that one time. Don't judge. Anthony was a real asshole and had it coming.

But then I thought about us going back to our apartments, and having nothing left but him. No matter how great the day was, no matter what we experienced, when the lights went down, the TV was turned off and the dark night set it, it was just him. It was only him.

The sinking feeling told me that this was all a waste of time. This whole adventure was a giant waste of time because we each had an Achilles heel of disconnection that he could exploit whenever he wanted.

We couldn't be with each other every second of every day. At some point, we'd let our guard down and he'd swoop in.

Once those tunnels are built, they're hard to escape from...except the way he shows you.

"Dude, don't give up", Binati said, appearing next to me in the booth.

"Binati?! I thought you couldn't leave the library! What are you doing here?"

"I'm on a tea break. Do they have tea in this place?"

"It's a BBQ joint. So they have sweet tea."

"Good God, man. Like I need more sugar during 2020. Fine, it'll have to do."

"Binati, seriously, you told me you couldn't come with me on this trip."

"Don't worry, man. Helen is holding down the fort. The library will be ok for a bit. I'm here to give you a little pep talk, you know?"

"I could use one right now."

"I know, that's why I'm here. Should I use some 80s material? You seem to like that."

"Nah. Not even a 'Police Academy' scene can help me now. I'll level with you; this whole thing feels like a disaster. A constant swim upstream. I feel like I'm gaining ground, then he swoops right in to remind me of the futility of everything. I feel exactly like I did back on that rooftop."

"That's because you're building a tunnel, don't you see? Do you think you're immune from those tunnels in this place? It can happen anywhere; even here. You need to break free, man. There's a lot more to do. You need to see it."

"Then just tell me and I'll do it."

"Don't be a lazy fuckshit. You know how these tales go. You're the hero of the story. You need to figure this out on your own. I'm just the sage or guide or Yoda or whatever who's here to nudge you along and kick you in the ass a bit to get there."

"Fair."

"But don't worry, I know what you're thinking and why you're starting to go down this path. I brought a book with me that will take you to a place that will help. It's called 'In the Heartland'. I think you'll really enjoy it."

"Ok. It couldn't hurt at this point. Tell me, how's Mel? Everyone else seems to be doing great in their missions, but I was a little concerned about her when I left her at the bar."

"Ready for the super cliche' answer?"

"Always."

"It will be revealed to you in time."

"Sweet. I knew you wouldn't disappoint."

"Speaking of sweet, they need to get that tea over here already. Do these people always move so slowly?"

"You're in the South. There isn't much of a sense of urgency here."

"You Americans are really something, you know."

You nodded when Binati said that. You knew the deal.

"Ok man, grab onto the book. It's time."

I took the book from Binati's hand and found myself immersed in it completely. Another vortex opened that sucked me in, and this time, the number 31 was appearing again, just like it did the first time I went through the poetry book with Ana-Maria.

The vortex accelerated me into what can only be described as a wide-open area where the sun was gently rising.

It was a vast cornfield in Indiana. It looked a lot like the opening scene from the movie *Hoosiers*.

I was half-expecting Gene Hackman to be driving by, sipping a cup of coffee.

I found myself outside a barn, on a large homestead that overlooked the fields. There were chickens, goats and pigs all around, but it was quiet. Incredibly quiet. Eerily quiet. It was even quieter than the Shadow's realm.

That was the oddest thing about all this.

Whenever I had a split-second of quiet, he'd show up. It seemed to be the case for everyone. When the mind is still, that's his cue.

And yet, he was nowhere to be found. I couldn't even sense him.

"That fucker won't show his face around here!", said Andrea, who was sitting in a chair outside the barn, smoking a cigarette while enjoying her coffee.

"Have a seat. Take a load off. Looks like you've had a rough morning."

Who was I to refuse such hospitality after a long... day? Eon? Who knew?

"Welcome to Indiana."

"Never been here before."

"I know. But you know all about Indiana. You know about us from the 90s when good 'ole number 31, Reggie Miller, would kick the crap out of your New York Knicks."

Again with the Reggie Miller references. Whoever dialed up this realm was clearly a big fan of 1990s NBA basketball.

"But this is *real* Indiana, man. This is the good stuff."

Andrea had a real sense of peace about her.

"How are you so relaxed sitting out here with such stillness?", I wondered, "He never lets me get a moment of quiet!"

"Oh, I know. You city types are all the same. Neurotic, nervous wrecks. He loves that shit. He thrives on it. He senses your anxiety like a raccoon sniffing around some old trash. Then ya'll don't stand a chance when he moves in for the kill, do you?"

"Not particularly. But you seem to have it all figured out."

"Man, I don't have shit figured out!"

She said that pretty authoritatively. It wasn't just small-town humility.

"Sean, look around dude."

I looked around. I saw corn. A lot of corn. A motherload of corn.

"What do you see?"

"Corn."

Andrea laughed.

"You would, wouldn't you. That's all you types ever see."

"Ok then, what is it? Magic corn?"

"Ain't nothing magical about this corn. Trust me on that. This harvest gives me lots of heartburn every year. But you know why it's special? It's special because it's mine. It's also yours. It definitely ain't his."

"What would he want with corn?"

"Same thing he wants with me. Same thing he wants with you. He doesn't want it to exist at all. He wants to tell you how it's all a big stupid hullabaloo about planting, growing and dying. But you see, it's so much more than that. We created this corn together. It grows as we grow. It dies as we die. And then it grows again. My son's going to take over this farm one day and keep it going...and there will be more corn. Then there will be even more after that."

"So, the purpose of life is corn?"

"Dude you're a real smart ass, anyone ever tell you that?"

"Once or twice."

"Yeah, Sarah warned me about you. So did Mel and Shanthi and the Mermaid."

"You know them, don't you?"

"Of course I know them."

"Was it them who saved you from 2020? Did they light your spark too? Did you light theirs the way they lit it for each other?"

"Dude, my spark's already lit. This corn lights it. These barn lights light it. Country living lights it. I don't need to see another face for the rest of my life and those sparks aren't going anywhere, trust me. Don't get me wrong, I love those ladies. I would take a fuckin' bullet for each of them, and would dish out plenty for them too, you can believe that. But I'm good right here."

"I don't understand. This isn't possible. Everything I've ever known has taught me that this bastard preys on the isolated, and that if you're disconnected, then he helps you build a tunnel to nothing. I've seen it with everyone."

"Well, that's right."

"Then explain this to me."

"Do you see me disconnected?"

"Yeah. You're all alone here."

"Am I? Ask yourself that question again. But before you do, I want you to close your eyes, take a deep breath, and look around. Ok?"

I did what she asked, and took a long, deep breath while closing my eyes. As this was happening, I started hearing a very faint humming sound.

"You hear that?"

"Yeah - what is that, Andrea?"

"They're talkin' to you."

"Who?"

"All of them."

I opened my eyes and saw faint sparks emanating from the outer borders of the barn, from the soil, from the corn, and from Andrea.

They were all connected.

"You see, I'm not alone. I'm never alone out here. I'm connected to the land. To the corn. To the fresh air. To the country. *That punk* can't touch me here. If he tries, I've got a loaded Remington pump-action 870 waiting for his bitch ass."

I wasn't sure how effective a shotgun would have been against the scourge of life as we knew it, but I appreciated the sentiment nonetheless.

"No offense, but you city people don't know a damn thing about a damn thing. You look around you and see our playground as hostile. You see everything as a threat. You see each other as threats. That sentiment just feeds off itself, until eventually, you really do become threats to each other. And you just end up doing all his damn work for him!"

"But isn't everything a threat? The drunk driver who killed my parents; what, did I just imagine that? This virus? Is none of this real?"

"It's all perception, man. Your version of real ain't my version of real. The only thing that's real is...well, everything. All that is...and that's ours. We just see it a bit differently from each other. It's what he's trying to take away, by convincing you that your jacked-up city perception is the only perception that's real. But he can't touch my country ass, and that's a fact!"

Andrea was sure of what she was saying. She was as confident in it as anyone I'd ever seen.

She seemed to have discovered something that eluded everyone else I'd met on this little bonanza...a way to battle him on her own.

With no other people needed to light her sparks. No pets. No friends. No hobbies. No business ideas.

Just stillness and a connection to all of creation, in all its various forms.

She created a wall of light around all of it.

Only, this wasn't a momentary flash. This wall was built to last like, a German engineered wall - seriously good craftsmanship.

Maybe this was the ticket?

Maybe this was the answer?

Maybe this was what I had been waiting for all along?

Maybe I should have stopped asking questions that began with 'maybe'?

This was the big reveal, it would seem.

Just being still, and being ok with all that is, was enough.

We didn't need all the extras...I mean, everything and everyone else was great and amazing and inspiring...but maybe just being ok with everything as it was...perhaps that was the answer?

Accepting that we all, somehow, created this together, and accepting this creation in all its flaws, instead of working with him to destroy it because it's not perfect?

Yet, as I had all these thoughts rolling through me, I couldn't help but shake a gnawing feeling.

A feeling of hollowness.

That, somehow, this wasn't the end-all, be-all answer.

I expected more finality.

Like, a grand parade for finally getting it right.

A throne room ceremony from *Star Wars* where there would be triumphant music and someone would put a medal around my neck and I'd growl like Chewbacca.

God, Chewy was the best, wasn't he?

Yet...I didn't feel anything.

I still felt incomplete.

"This isn't enough for you, is it?", Andrea asked.

"I'm sorry, but it isn't."

"You got nothing to be sorry about. This isn't your last stop, bubba. We just needed you to see this so you knew it was possible. We wanted you to see a different element of connection that you hadn't seen before."

"So, there's more?"

"Let me tell you this, there's always more. Always."

I knew she was right. But I still felt like I was at a dead end.

"Andrea, it's been real. Thank you for everything. But I need to go."

"I know. It's time."

I had to go back to the library.

Maybe there were more books to grab, more adventures to go on, more people to meet.

If this wasn't the end, I'm sure Binati and Helen could give me another path. Something else to follow.

To keep this going a little while longer until I found the ways to bring the resistance all together.

To get us on the same page.

To create a unified front.

To get everyone out of 2020.

To fight him until the end.

I closed my eyes and clinched my fists, focusing intently on getting back to the library.

I tried conjuring up a phone booth for one more awesome Bill and Ted ride, but it wouldn't appear.

I tried summoning a vortex to get me there, but that wouldn't appear either.

Instead, I started to see everything around me begin to pixelate, like when there's a really spotty wi-fi connection.

Andrea. The cornfields. The sky. Hell, even the goats.

Pixilation everywhere. It felt like an eternal process that I was lost inside of.

Then the pixilation finally completed.

And all that was left…was nothing.

Absolutely nothing at all.

"*Welcome home*", he said, appearing next to me, "Your *real home.*"

I looked right at him, and he looked right at me.

It was the longest, coldest stare of my life.

"*Welcome to* the *end.*"

Chapter 12: THE FINAL DESTINATION

Nothing.

Just…nothing.

When we conceive of nothing, we think of everything being entirely dark. We imagine a place that resembles Space, but without the luminescent stars.

That's as far as the human mind can stretch to conceive of this concept. We quite literally have no ability to comprehend it otherwise.

All we see is a vast, unendingly dark expanse.

But this place wasn't that. This was something else. I know it may sound like a bit of a cop-out, but I can't find the words to describe this to you.

Not being able to tell you about this place hurts the most because this was the part of the journey where you left me.

After everything faded to nothing, you faded with it.

You were gone.

You were so completely and utterly gone.

In the last place the Shadow took me, that Siberian-type place, you were faintly there like an echo, a specter of some kind. But here, there was no one, not even you. In the strangest way possible, he wasn't here either; at least, not as I knew him.

I always knew him as something that stood apart from everything. There was something, and then there was him. It was two separate, distinct entities.

This place though...here...whatever this is, which I don't even think is really a place...was him.

This was what the inside of the Shadow himself looked like.

It was neither warm nor cold, like the other place he took me. I felt neither apprehensive, nor at ease.

I felt nothing. I was nothing...just like him.

All I had left was a faint remnant of my consciousness, that I felt was starting to gradually slip away too.

"You tried, didn't you?" he asked.

"I did. With everything I had."

"I respect that. Most don't keep up the fight against me that long. Most throw in the towel. Most, even the ones with the most vitality, eventually understand the futility of it. They simply stop trying. They give in. They realize that what you see around you right now is what was always waiting for them."

"But I was there. I saw them. They may not have been organized under the banner of a 'resistance' as Binati showed me in that book, but...that was real. They were real. They fought you with everything they had."

"Of course they did. For the time they had. However, when their time was over, others tried to pick up the baton. Some succeeded for a while too. Then they passed it onto others. This continued for longer than you can conceive of right now. But it was eventually over. It all led here."

"Why did you bring me here? To show me what was waiting?"

"I didn't bring you here. I've never taken you anywhere. Ana-Maria was right when she told you about this in Spain. You sent yourself there. You went on this entire journey on your own. Your perception needed to see this play out, so you could come back here and confirm that which you always suspected."

"Which is what?"

"The utter pointlessness of it all. Here, let's take a little tour, shall we? It's your decision, of course."

"Ok."

I felt my senses starting to come back, just a bit, particularly my sense of sight.

Then I saw them. I saw silhouettes; vague, Shadowy things started to appear, and they seemed to tell stories.

I saw the story of Ana-Maria and Kelsey. I saw their art expo. I saw their smiling faces. I saw their art light up the spark. I saw it spark creativity and light. I saw it spark connections all over the world. I saw artists creating digital expos to get them through lockdowns. Then I saw it all fade. I saw it pixelate. I saw the art disintegrate. I saw the paintings wither, and I saw the creative spark that drove it slowly burn out…until it became one with this place.

I saw Helen and Binati welcome millions of visitors into the library. I saw the sparks of imagination light up the faces of children, and I saw them grow up to write more books, which they returned to the library, which were read by other children, who grew up to write books of their own. I saw what had to have been thousands of generations pass through this ritual. Then, the numbers slowly dwindled. There were less books written, less read, and eventually, the library closed and later disintegrated into nothingness and just disappeared.

I saw college football eventually disbanded as the models for the sport and universities changed over time, and Fitz and Keith gradually lost their connections to the game, to each other, and to everyone else who was associated with it. I saw the Liverpool and Chennai fans suffer the same fate over time.

Hundreds of years were condensed into a blink, yet I saw it all. Every minute. Every detail.

I saw the love in the eyes of Greg and Judy turn to pain and grief when Judy lost Greg. I saw the love Violeta had for Puppa turn into that same grief when it was Puppa's time to go too. It was unbearable to watch.

I asked him to stop, but he told me how he couldn't turn this off, since he wasn't the one who turned it on.

This was my private viewing. I'm the one who pressed "play". This was something that I, somehow, wanted to see.

This is what I'd wanted to see all along.

Then I saw Mel, the Mermaid and Shanthi.

"Please, make this stop", I begged him, "I can't see what comes next. I can't do this."

He didn't say a word.

I knew what I was about to witness. I knew I was going to see them die.

I was going to see a grief that was unimaginable to me; one even worse than when I lost Nana.

I was going to witness a mother lose her daughters again, and her daughters lose their mother.

I was overwhelmed with what few senses I had left. But pain was the most powerful among them.

This was a pain unlike anything I'd ever felt.

Why, goddamnit, WHY?

Why was I putting myself through this?

I saw the living room scene again. The tearful embrace when they took the first step towards each other. The moment when they'd found each other across time and space. The moment they began the work of completing each other.

I saw the sparks. I somehow felt the warmth again, even here.

But I was nervously anticipating what would come next.

The dissolution of everything. The fraying of bonds. Each of them returning to 2020 in their own way.

I wasn't ready for it. I couldn't bear the thought.

But...that's not what I saw.

Not at all.

Instead of a return to 2020, I saw rebirth.

I saw them take that one extra step into the light. They took an extra step towards each other.

I saw Shanthi telling Mel that it was ok to mourn the loss of everything. It was ok to feel it taken from her. This right there was the birth of a new connection. She could fill the hole in her heart, the one left by the death of her family and the end of the conventions, with their love. All she needed was to take one more step to release the anguish once and for all, and let the Mermaid and Shanthi simply be there for her.

She didn't need the conventions to make her whole. She simply needed to allow herself to be accepted for the first time in her life. She needed to realize, with their help, how she was enough.

Mel dug deep, reached with everything she had, grabbed onto the one last ounce of light she had left, and took the step.

She did it. She went all-in. She joined them…and I saw sparks around her like I'd never seen around anyone before.

The Mermaid was next, and she needed to see it too. She needed to take that one extra step to realize the fact that the curse of the Mermaid never actually existed. She needed to realize, with their help, how she too was enough. She let the love in this room remind her of that. She was forced to release the self-hatred that had consumed her all the days of her life, and follow the prophecy of Mr. C that led her to this place. She had to allow herself, for the first time in her life, to simply be ok.

The Mermaid took the step too, and her sparks went all over the place, just like Mel's.

It all started in this living room. I didn't realize it at the time. It was all connected. The present, future and past. This wasn't a linear journey. Mel stepping into this light changed the course of her existence. And it changed the Mermaid's too. Allowing herself to let go is what propelled the Mermaid on this journey of hers.

She couldn't heal the others until she was first healed herself.

Once she accepted herself, she was able to do more. She was able to reach the others. She managed to fulfill this mission of hers.

Watching this scene unfold, Shanthi lit up as well. She found her motherly glow, and found her purpose again. She stood tall, no longer ashamed by what she couldn't provide her family, but rather proud of who she was, the souls she comforted, the impact she created and the goodness she spread.

…and now, they were reaching out to me, bringing me back to that moment in the living room…the moment they asked me to join them.

The moment I turned away and demanded more answers.

The moment that brought me to him.

But now, I begged my old self not to make the same mistake twice.

I told the old me to let the light of the three of them illuminate me. I wanted to join them all.

"Fuck him! Fuck the Shadow!", I yelled at myself in the silhouette, through choked back tears, as I saw my old self retreating from Mel, Shanthi and the Mermaid, "Fuck your answers! Fuck your mission! Fuck your quest! Just go to them, goddamnit! Just go to them! They're begging you. Just go. Please. Just go. Don't say no this time. Just go!"

The silhouette of the old me paused, as if he'd heard something he couldn't put his finger on.

"JUST GO! GO TO THEM!"

Somehow, in that moment, I knew.

I knew everything.

That was the pivotal moment.

That was the essence of this entire experience.

That one singular embrace.

That was all that was, all that is, and all that ever will be.

It all manifested in that one perfect moment.

It was pure love. Pure connection. It was home. It was my real home.

My home wasn't this desolate place. Joining them was the ultimate act of resistance. This resistance was called self-love, self-acceptance, vulnerability, letting it all go, and releasing everything, once and for all.

It was about embracing the fact that creation was not a mistake. It was something I was a part of. As imperfect as it was. As painful as it could be. It was mine. It was theirs. It was ours. Joining them would be the ultimate affirmation of that.

"Don't do this", the Shadow said, suddenly getting very agitated.

"GO! GO TO THEM!"

"I'm warning you. You have no idea what you're about to unleash. You can't change one thing without changing everything else. Your perception has governed the course of your entire existence here. It's been one sequence of events that you've been able to interpret. That you've been able to wrap your mind around. Your quest for answers always led you to me, don't you see?

You weren't looking for answers. You thought you were. You were really looking for me. For certainty. I provided you with that - certainty.

Everything you encountered, everyone you've met, it was just another stone in the long road to me. To here. It was all one long tunnel.

You could have escaped any time you wanted. You could have left 2020 in that living room. You could have left it by remaining at the Winery. You could have left it by remaining on that elephant in the Serengeti. But each time, you chose to remain in 2020."

"The hell I did! I was trying to find the resistance to you! The freedom fighters to liberate us from 2020. To stand up for what we created."

"You were already liberated. Each of them liberated you. You were liberated through humor, love and friendship. But you refused to remove your chains. You kept them on and continued searching.

Each one of them was your ticket out. Yet you chose to keep searching for me, because I'm the only one who can provide you answers.

This thing you've all created...it has no meaning. It has no ultimate purpose. To quote Harmeet, 'It's chaos'. You will never find your answers there. You will only find them with me. That's why the end of your journey brought you here."

"What will happen if I change it? What will happen? Tell me. What happens if I join with them in that living room?"

He was really getting angry now.

"Don't do it. I'm warning you."

"Tell me, damn it! What happens if I join them??"

The energy between the two of us was starting to build up dramatically, filling the void with a chaotic swirling of different patterns, shapes and colors.

"You really want to know?"

"YES! WHAT HAPPENS?"

"Your friend wins."

"What friend??"

"The one who's always fought me over you. The one who's never left your side. The one who's been with you on this entire journey. The one who encouraged you to take this journey in the first place. The one who helped you manifest this entire thing. The one who's seen this entire thing through your eyes. The one who's lived this with you. The one who's created this with you as you've gone along. The one who's listening in on this right now. The one who's following every single word we're speaking to each other."

You.

It was you.

It was always you.

You have been my companion on this journey.

You have been the one inspiring me the entire way.

You're the one who wanted me to experience this, who wanted me to immerse, who wanted me to learn.

You've been his counterpart this entire time.

You've been his foil.

You're the one who's brought the light to me.

You're the reason I fought him on that wrestling playground.

You're the reason why I took this journey to find new ways to fight him.

You wanted me to find some hope.

You wanted me to find a brighter path.

You wanted me to find something that could inspire others.

You wanted me to find these answers.

...Because you wanted to leave 2020 too.

You wanted to find a way out alongside me.

You wanted to release me, as well as yourself, from his grip.

So you accompanied me. You encouraged me. You hoped I'd find some revelation that could help you as well...perhaps light your spark as well.

...so that you may light others.

I understood. I knew.

I took this journey...for the sole purpose of understanding the light.

You're the one who lit my spark.

You're the one who's always lit my spark.

The energy was now swirling around in a frantic uncontrollable way, as he yelled, "Stop! If you do this, everything in your perception will collapse. Your tunnel will cave in on you. And you won't recognize what comes next! Your friend won't remember any of this! You're tied together in this! If you go, so do they!"

"Why? Why would my friend not remember this?"

"Because your friend facilitated this journey for you. Your friend, like me, exists within you. Your friend saw this journey and helped you facilitate it. From beginning to end. If you alter it, your friend's part of this saga will vanish. And it will all have been for nothing."

I understood what he meant. My heart was racing. I knew that if I joined them in that living room...if I allowed myself to be taken in by them, if I softened my heart, if I stopped searching for answers, if I allowed myself to leave 2020 that way, it would blow everything else up. Including us. And your memory of this.

But I had to do it.

This was my moment. This was my time. I'd waited my whole life to break him.

So I screamed with everything I had, "DO IT! JOIN THEM!"

The silhouette of my old self released himself from the vortex that was dragging him into the Shadow's realm, and he joined the explosion of light created by Mel, the Mermaid and Shanthi.

When he joined them, he started exploding with sparks and the light beamed out in every direction, breaking through the silhouette and into this realm of nothing. The nothing was filled with light. It was filled with love. It was filled with gratitude. It was filled with family.

It was intense and powerful and explosive. It was as if all of creation was manifesting before my eyes. I felt the strength of pure energy, of everyone's pure energy, coursing through me.

And then...

...I saw an apparition of Nana appear. She was in the light with us. I saw my parents. They were in the light too.

I saw Richie. I saw everyone who'd been transformed into pure light.

I felt them. I felt them all. Their thoughts. Their hopes. Their dreams.

I was one with them. I was one with everything.

The light overwhelmed me and overwhelmed everything.

It sparked an even brighter flash that I wasn't able to contain, something that was so powerful it's beyond anyone's ability to even comprehend.

The light blinded me. I couldn't see anyone anymore. Or anything. He was long gone. So was everyone else. It was now a blinding flash.

It was pure, vibrating energy.

That's it.

Just pure, raw energy.

I lived in that energy for what felt like an eternity.

A true, actual eternity.

This was it. I was really one with everything now.

I had truly crossed over. I had truly won.

But then...the energy gradually gave way to another round of pixilation, and suddenly things began to take form again.

I lost my grip on eternity and the vibrating energy began to solidify.

Piece by piece, shape by shape, sense by sense.

I begged to hang on. I didn't want to leave the light. I'd never known anything as perfect. I held on with everything I could.

But it was no use.

I was slipping away. Everything began to form again. Everything I perceived as real reappeared.

...and that's how I ended up back here.

Slowly regaining my consciousness.

Starting to see things fade back into being.

Fading back...onto my rooftop.

...on the ledge.

...ready to jump.

...and sitting next to you again.

You're giving me a blank stare right now, as if you had just heard this all for the first time.

Somehow, talking myself into joining their collective of light managed to wipe your memory of what happened, just as he predicted.

Now...we are both back in 2020.

We're here again, right back where this all started.

And yet...I remember.

I remember everything.

Despite being back on this ledge, I feel still, I feel ok.

I don't see him anywhere, and this is usually his cue to show up.

He was certainly here last time.

But as I look out onto the street, onto the rotting stacks of garbage and litter and wino's...I feel strangely ok.

I think I know what Andrea meant now, if there even was an Andrea.

This street is my cornfield. This building is my barn.

I feel the stillness, accept it, and...and he's not here.

It's just peaceful, somehow. It's just as it should be. Despite being in 2020. Despite being locked down. It's somehow all ok.

Maybe I was meant to leave 2020 that way; whichever way that was.

If I ever even left at all.

Now, I'm sure he'll be back one day.

Sabriya and Brian and Edna were right - you can't beat him. You can only fight him.

I have to accept that. As Greg said, it's the price of admission we all pay.

So tonight, I fight him with the stillness.

Andrea, thank you, my friend. Wherever and whatever you are.

I fight him for the sake of the others. Mel...if there even was a Mel...I won't let you down. I promise you. I'll do whatever I can to get these conventions back one day. If not for you, then for the others. Maybe I'll start a blog and write about it.

But still, after all that, where does this leave me now?

Well, whatever it meant, I do know one thing.

Tomorrow morning, I'm going to take a stroll on the East side of the park on 59th, watch the sunrise, and see what might be waiting for me.

Maybe in that sunrise, I can grab onto a piece of that light again. Even a small piece...and, with it, perhaps a new possibility.

As for you, I wish you could remember; just a small part of it because I have to find the light again somehow. You were the only one who was there with me when I found it.

Maybe we can find it together?

Maybe enough time will pass, and you'll remember your connection to the light if only to tell me this wasn't all in my head.

Perhaps we can leave 2020 together. You and me.

Perhaps you can find a spark that makes you remember the journey; a spark that gets you out of here too.

Maybe you can...

...wait...hold up.

I feel my phone buzzing...but I remember throwing it off the roof before this all happened.

This doesn't make any sense. How is my phone back in my pocket again?

Should I check it this time?

What have I got to lose? Where am I going, right?

Hmm.

That's odd.

Really odd.

A LinkedIn notification?

I haven't been on that platform in months.

Should I check it out?

Yeah?

You think so?

Ok, why not at this point...

Let's see...an invitation to a Mindset Zoom with some folks around the world also dealing with lockdown.

Mindset Zoom?

The invitation is from Mirrie Mac.

Mirrie Mac?

Who the hell is Mirrie Mac? Like I said, I barely come on this platform.

Let me magnify her picture a bit.

Let's see if I can...

...oh.

Oh my God.

No...this...no...

This is impossible.

This can't be.

Mirrie Mac...

...is the Mermaid.

The Mermaid.

"What's your mindset?"

Oh my God.

This was her mission.

They're real.

They're all real.

...and they're here.

ABOUT THE AUTHOR

Geoff Woliner, founder of Winning Wit, has spent the last decade helping people from all walks of life tell their stories to the world through book writing, speech writing, copy writing and presentation coaching.

Geoff is the author of "Get Bitter to Get Better: How to reclaim your confidence, prove your villains wrong, and win the big moments in life", "The Gen X Code: How to keep your cool during the Coronavirus and other things that suck", and "The Adventures of SuperJay, Wall Street Crusader."

He created the character of Sean Gallo as an amalgamation of his own battles with the Shadow, and those of people near and dear to him who still live in New York.

Follow Geoff's Author page for links to his other publications and updates on his latest blog, vlog and podcast content.

If this book spoke to you and helped along your own journey, please leave a review!

Thank you for taking this adventure with us, and may you also leave 2020 and find your own perma-spark along the way.

"Literary Device"

Made in the USA
Monee, IL
10 December 2020